W9-CHE-764

Wish You
Were Here,
Liza
SUMMER
APPLE
CANDY

This book belongs to
MS. MEIKRANTZ

candy apple books... just for you.

The Accidental Cheerleader by Mimi McCoy

The Boy Next Door by Laura Dower

Miss Popularity by Francesco Sedita

How to Be a Girly Girl in Just Ten Days
by Lisa Papademetriou

Drama Queen by Lara Bergen

The Babysitting Wars by Mimi McCoy

Totally Crushed by Eliza Willard

I've Got a Secret by Lara Bergen

Callie for President by Robin Wasserman

Making Waves by Randi Reisfeld and H.B. Gilmour

The Sister Switch
by Jane B. Mason and Sarah Hines Stephens

Accidentally Fabulous by Lisa Papademetriou

Confessions of a Bitter Secret Santa by Lara Bergen

Accidentally Famous by Lisa Papademetriou

Star-Crossed by Mimi McCoy

Accidentally Fooled by Lisa Papademetriou

Miss Popularity Goes Camping by Francesco Sedita

Life, Starring Me! by Robin Wasserman

Juicy Gossip by Erin Downing

Accidentally Friends by Lisa Papademetriou

Snowfall Surprise
by Jane B. Mason and Sarah Hines Stephens

The Sweetheart Deal by Holly Kowitt

Rumor Has It by Jane B. Mason and Sarah Hines Stephens

Super Sweet 13 by Helen Perelman

Wish You Were Here, Liza

SUMMER • CANDY APPLE •

by Robin Wasserman

SCHOLASTIC INC.

New York Toronto London Auckland
Sydney Mexico City New Delhi Hong Kong

For Susie, who taught me how to make grilled cheese sandwiches over the campfire and didn't get mad that time I almost drove us off a cliff.

ISBN 978-0-545-17222-6

12 11 10 9 8 7 6 5 4 3 2 1 10 11 12 13 14 15/0

Printed in the U.S.A. 40
First printing, May 2010

Chapter One

Location: 35,000 feet above Ohio
Population: 347 passengers, 23 flight attendants, 2 pilots, 1 yapping Chihuahua in the carrier under the seat behind me
Miles Driven: 0
Days of Torment: 1

"In the event of an emergency landing, your seat cushion can be used as a flotation device," the flight attendant announced as we took off.

I wanted to raise my hand. *I have an emergency*, I would have said.

I'm on the wrong plane.

On the wrong trip.

In the wrong family.

Stuck in the wrong summer.

Just lend me a parachute, I would have said, *and I'll get out of your way.*

I used to like airplanes. The taking-off part was fun, like a lame amusement park ride. The food was gross, but there was always dessert — cookies or pretzels or candy bars — and, unlike at home, I was allowed to have as much as I wanted. There were people to eavesdrop on, bad movies to watch, and, if I was lucky, a pair of gold wings that I could pin to my backpack. It was pretty much the greatest thing ever.

At least, that's what I thought when I was a kid.

Turns out I was kind of a dumb kid.

Don't get me wrong. The plane wasn't the problem. Not the *whole* problem, at least. Yes, it smelled like BO. Yes, lunch was two pieces of stale bread with watery mustard smushed between them. (There was no way I was going to eat any of the other stuff they gave us.) Yes, the Chihuahua in the carrying case shoved under the seat behind me *Would. Not. Stop. Barking.* But I could have handled all that. *If* we'd been flying somewhere acceptable. Like Hawaii. Or Florida.

Or home.

I closed my eyes, trying to imagine that.

If I were home, I'd be at the local pool, stretching out in the sun, wondering whether Lucas McKidd would notice my new purple bathing suit. Or I'd be figuring out what to wear on the first day of camp. A counselor-in-training had to look the part. I would make my best friends, Sam and Mina, come over and —

That's where the fantasy cut off, like someone unplugged the power cord. Even if I *were* home, Sam and Mina wouldn't be there. Mina was at art camp and Sam was at the beach. They were both away for the whole summer — just like me.

"Liza, we have a surprise for you!" my mom had said, peeking her head into my room the day after my birthday. My father peered over her shoulder.

That should have been my first clue. If it had been a *good* surprise, they would have given it to me *on* my birthday, right? Instead of a new calculator and ten rolls of film for the decrepit, non-digital camera that I'd been begging them to replace.

My second clue? Surprises in my family are almost never a good thing.

Surprise . . . we're going to eat nothing but tofu and kale for dinner this month!

Surprise . . . Great-aunt Marge is coming to stay with us for two weeks, and you *get to share your bedroom with her!*

Surprise . . .

"We're going on a family vacation — for the *whole* summer!" my mother announced, eyes glowing. My father beamed. I buried my head under my pillow, hoping I was still asleep.

I wasn't.

When I came downstairs, my parents were in the living room, already planning the Great Gold Family Summer Vacation. All *two months* of it. We would fly to Chicago, rent a car, and spend the rest of the summer driving across "this amazing country of ours, seeing whatever there is to see." (That was my father, digging through a mound of travel guides.) It would be a "once-in-a-lifetime adventure that none of us will ever forget." (That was my mother, already making a list of "World's Largest" tourist traps she wanted to hit: World's Largest Bottle of Catsup. World's Largest van Gogh Painting. The whole trip was sounding like the World's Largest Disaster.) "And once we get to California, we'll spend three days at the beach, just for *you*," my father concluded. Like three days at the beach would make up for *two months* of torment.

No amount of yelling, pouting, crying, or sulking changed their minds. It didn't matter that this was supposed to be my first summer as a CIT (not that I loved little kids or anything, but what did being a CIT have to do with liking little kids?). It didn't matter that all my friends would be here having fun without me (except Sam and Mina, but that wasn't the point). It didn't matter that I was starting seventh grade in the fall, which meant this was the perfect summer for a perfect first kiss (not that I told my parents *that*). It didn't matter that the absolute, very last thing in the entire world I would ever want to do was spend two months *trapped in a car with my parents.* All that mattered was that they wanted to go.

We went.

* * *

Location: Cheap-O Car Rental, Chicago, IL
Population: 2.8 million
Miles Driven: 0
Days of Torment: 1 (felt like 100)

There were a few small problems with the Great Gold Family Summer Vacation. For one thing, there was nothing great about it. For another, it wasn't technically a Gold family vacation. At least, it wasn't *just* the Gold family.

Before I was born, my parents joined CRAWL, the Champions of Real America and its WonderLands. They had a fancy website and an official motto ("This land is your land"). But really it was just a bunch of people from all over the country who liked going on weird vacations to weird spots, like the National Presidential Wax Museum (Keystone, South Dakota) or the World's Largest Ball of Twine (Darwin, Minnesota).

When I was little, we went on a lot of trips with my parents' two favorite CRAWL families, the Kaplan-Novaks and the Schwebers. We went to Reptiland (Allenwood, Pennsylvania) where there was a machine that let you feed live crickets to a pet turtle. We made a pilgrimage to Mr. Muffles (Acushnet, Massachusetts), which was a roadside statue made out of old motorcycle parts. Three statues, actually: a man, his dog, and a fire hydrant. (You can guess what the dog was doing.) We saw the Whispering Statue in Barre, Vermont; the Snowmobile Museum in Allenstown, New Hampshire; and Frank Sinatra's used pink hand towel in Atlantic City, New Jersey, only an hour away from home. And then my mom switched jobs, I went to camp, and for a few years we didn't go anywhere at all.

It was bliss.

But now that family vacation was back, the Kaplan-Novaks and the Schwebers were back, too. And so were their kids.

We met them at the car rental place by the airport. The office was as old and crumbly as the guy behind the counter. While my parents filled out forms for our rental car, I grabbed a paper cup of lukewarm water and ducked outside. The Kaplan-Novaks were waiting. I hadn't seen them in four years, but they were exactly like I remembered. Professor Novak had more hair on his face than on his head, and a permanently impatient expression, like he was bored with his whole life. His wife, Professor Kaplan, wore a red tracksuit and a black headband. It was the kind of thing you wore when you wanted to *look* like you were dressing casual. But there was nothing casual about Professor Kaplan. Even though they'd come all the way from North Carolina, her hair was perfectly smooth and glossy. Her makeup wasn't even smudged.

I wiped a sleeve across my sweaty forehead and tried to smooth down my frizz.

She gave me a thin smile. "Liza, I assume?"

I nodded.

"You've grown," she said with faint surprise, like she couldn't believe I'd done something right. Then she nodded at the two girls standing at her side. "You remember Dillie and Kirsten, of course?"

The Kirsten I remembered wore thick glasses and baggy overalls, kept her eyes on the ground and her voice to a whisper. But this Kirsten was just as pretty and polished as her mother, with wavy blond hair rippling over a glasses-free face. She was only four years older than me, but she looked like she was already in college. She gave me a fake smile, then rolled her eyes and went back to texting on her cell phone.

"Say hello to your friend, Dillie," Professor Kaplan urged her other daughter. Dillie was my age, not that she looked it. She wore a neon-green sweatshirt with a hot pink planet plastered across the front. A moon-shaped pendant hung around her neck, and oversize green alien earrings dangled beneath her wild blond hair. I couldn't imagine going out in public like that — not on purpose, at least. (I still had nightmares about the day I accidentally wore my teddy bear pajama shirt to school.)

Professor Kaplan nudged Dillie toward me. "You two kids catch up. Your father and I are going to go deal with this car situation."

"Don't forget, you said I could drive, too!" Kirsten said, without looking up from her phone.

Professor Kaplan and Professor Novak exchanged a glance, then sighed. They stepped into the car rental office, Kirsten hot on their heels. My "friend" and I were left alone.

"Isn't this awesome?" Dillie said.

I looked around. There were junky cars, tired tourists, heat waves rising from the black cement — but definitely no awesomeness. "Um, what?"

"This!" Dillie rocked back and forth on the balls of her feet. "I've been so psyched for this trip. I can't believe we get to go away for the *whole* summer. It'll be just like the old days." She tapped her backpack. "I spent the whole flight reading about Route 66. Like, did you know it crosses eight states and three time zones? And we're going to see them *all*! Awesome, right?"

"Right. Totally." I was starting to get that feeling in my stomach. Like last summer at the amusement park when I'd eaten one too many bags of cotton candy.

"Of course, Roswell — that's Roswell, New Mexico, UFO capital of the world — it's not actually *on* Route 66, but Naomi and Peter — that's my mom and dad; I call them Naomi and Peter, or sometimes Professor Kaplan and Professor Novak, which is kind of a joke, except they don't think it's funny. Anyway, they promised we could take a side trip to Roswell. Won't that be cool?"

You never know, Mina had told me at our "See Ya Soon" party. (Because best friends never say "good-bye.") *Maybe you'll like them.*

Yeah, Sam had added. *You might decide to trade us in for new best friends.*

You've got nothing *to worry about*, I thought, missing them already. Sam, Mina, and I had promised to mail one another souvenirs, but I wouldn't get mine until the end of the summer. (Since we were going to be moving from motel to motel almost every night, there was no way for me to get mail until we arrived in California.) No cell phones and no e-mail meant that I wouldn't hear from them anytime before that. How was I supposed to get through a whole summer without my best friends?

"So, have you seen Caleb yet?" Dillie asked eagerly. (I was starting to remember that Dillie said everything eagerly.)

I shook my head, just as a silver SUV pulled up to the curb. The front doors opened, and Mr. and Mrs. Schweber climbed out, looking pretty much the same as they used to. Very thin, very quiet, very beige. I couldn't see Caleb through the tinted back window, which gave me a moment to hope.

Maybe he'll be cute! Sam had pointed out. *The two of you together, all summer long; you never know . . .*

Sam and Mina were convinced that Caleb would turn out to be my one true love. Sure, the Caleb I remembered was a short, shy, neat-freak, kind of lost inside his own head, but that was a long time ago. We hadn't seen each other since we were eight years old. Everything was different now, and maybe Caleb would turn out to be . . .

. . . exactly the same as when we were eight.

Same height, same clothes, same goofy smile. He climbed out of the SUV and pushed his glasses up on his face. He looked like Harry Potter. And *not* the cute movie version.

"Hey, Dillie," he mumbled. He gave us both a limp wave. "Hey, Lizard."

I leaned forward, hoping I'd heard him wrong. "Did you say —"

"Lizard!" Dillie squealed. "How'd I forget about that?"

"It's *Liza*," I said firmly. "*Not* Lizard."

Dillie grinned. "Whatever you say, Lizard."

When Caleb didn't say anything, she gave him a friendly shove. "Yeah, *Lizard*," he added. He smiled shyly at Dillie, like he was waiting for a gold star. "Whatever you say."

Before I could explain to them that they were not, under any circumstances, to call me *Lizard* ever again, Dillie's parents filed out of the rental place. Mine came out a moment later, followed by Kirsten. The adults were all chattering to one another about how exciting this was, how long it had been, how they couldn't wait to hit the road, blah blah blah. . . . I stopped listening. I just stared out at the strip of highway that wound around the rental place, wondering how I was going to survive for fifty-four more days. I pulled out my camera and snapped a picture of the road. *The beginning of the torment*, I thought, assigning it an invisible caption.

And because I was peering through the camera lens, counting the cars driving by, I didn't see the SUV door open again.

"Come on, Jake," someone said. "You'll have plenty of time to listen to the game once we get back on the road. Come out here and meet everybody."

"Hey, everybody," a low voice said. "I'm Jake. Guess you figured that."

I turned around — and almost dropped my camera.

I felt like I was at the amusement park again. But this time, it wasn't the too-much-cotton-candy feeling. It was that top-of-the-roller-coaster, stomach-clenching, scary-exciting, make-you-want-to-throw-your-hands-in-the-air-and-scream feeling.

"This is our nephew, Jake," Mr. Schweber said. "His parents thought he might like to see a little of the country. Isn't that right, Jake?"

Jake shrugged. "Whatever."

Sam and Mina aren't going to believe this, I thought.

He was *cute*. No, that's not right. He wasn't cute at all — he was handsome. Like, TV-star handsome. Bright blue eyes, shaggy brown hair, broad shoulders, and you could just tell he would have an incredible smile, even though he wasn't smiling. That was the best part. . . . He looked just as bored as I felt. It was obvious he didn't want to be here any more than I did.

It was starting to look like maybe, just maybe, this trip wouldn't be so bad after all.

Chapter Two

Location: Collinsville, Illinois
Population: 24,707
Miles Driven: 612 (the 251.7 miles between Chicago and Collinsville, plus the 360.3 miles spent meandering aimlessly along every highway, byway, and gravel road in eastern Illinois)
Days of Torment: 6

It turned out the trip wasn't as bad as I expected.

It was worse.

Caleb's cute cousin was fourteen, from Philadelphia, and liked baseball. Those were all the details I learned — and I had to learn them from Caleb. Because "I'm Jake" turned out to be pretty much the only thing Jake had to say. After he introduced himself, he stuck his earbuds in his ears and went back to listening to a baseball game. He didn't take them out again for the rest of the day. Or the next day.

Some of my friends had been to Chicago before. According to them, it was pretty cool. I wouldn't know. We skipped Chicago completely. Who would want to hang out in a big city, full of restaurants and movie theaters and Internet cafés, when you could spend your days on a dusty road, driving past abandoned gas stations and giant rock quarries? We were supposed to be seeing the "real" America.

But what was so real about the World's Largest Catsup Bottle? Or Johnny's Route 66 Cafe?

The café, an hour's drive from the giant water tower painted to look like a bottle of catsup, was built in 1937. I was pretty sure it hadn't gotten a new paint job — or a new food shipment — since opening day. I poked at the stale bread on my turkey sandwich, trying to figure out if the green stuff along one edge was "Johnny's special sauce" or mold. The little restaurant was crammed with retro Route 66–themed stuff, like road signs and license plates and broken neon letters spelling out FO_D in blinking lights.

"Check it out," Dillie said, pointing at the 1950s movie posters hanging over our heads. They all featured multiheaded green aliens peeking out of retro spaceships, with taglines like, THEY CAME IN PEACE . . . BUT STAYED FOR WAR. "Wait till we get to Roswell," Dillie said. (Eagerly.) "I bet the whole *town* is like this."

I gave her the rest of my fries and went outside to see if there was anything interesting to take a picture of. Or anything interesting, period. No such luck . . . just road. So I took (yet another) picture of that. Every once in a while, a car sped past at ninety miles an hour. *Why so eager to get from one side of nowhere to the other?* I wondered, trying to get the red smear of a convertible on film. Though I had to admit, it sounded better than being stuck in the middle. Like us.

That was the day we hit our first big tourist "hotspot": Cahokia Mounds, the site of an ancient civilization called the Mississippians. (I wondered why they weren't called the Illinois-ians, but I didn't wonder enough to ask.) I'd been picturing something like the Mayan ruins we'd learned about in school, lots of cool pyramids and temples.

But the Cahokia Mounds were just . . . *mounds.* Large, grassy lumps. Some were ten feet tall, some were a hundred, but none was anything more than a mound of dirt. I snapped a picture of one of the smaller lumps. As usual, I gave it an imaginary caption: *Proof that the past was just as boring as the present.*

Dillie tugged at me and Caleb. "Race you to the top!" she cried, charging toward the tallest mound without waiting to see if we would follow.

"Come on," Caleb urged me. He ran after her.

It was one of those warm, sunny summer days that just made you feel like running. "Hurry up, Lizard!" Dillie shouted over her shoulder. "What are you waiting for?"

Lizard. I grimaced. If they were going to insist on using that nickname, then let them race without me. Instead, I followed the adults into the "Interpretive Center." Jake had disappeared somewhere, as usual, but Kirsten stuck by her parents' side, acting totally superior. Also as usual.

The Interpretive Center was sort of like a museum, only less interesting. The walls were lined with photographs of the mounds, like we couldn't just look out the window and see them. One display had drawings of what the ancient Mississippian city might have looked like, back when there were still ancient Mississippians. Another had a bunch of archaeological artifacts under glass: an old spoon, an old bowl, a bunch of old rocks. I wondered what the archaeologists of the future would find when they dug up the musty remains of my bedroom. A thousand-year-old copy of *Bring It On*? What a legacy.

"About a thousand years ago, this place was the biggest city in the world," Kirsten said, loud enough to make sure that the nearest Interpretive Center staffer would hear her. (She was quoting the brochure, but she made it sound like she'd learned about all this a long time ago.)

The staffer smiled eagerly at Kirsten. "Very good," he said, gesturing us over to a large map of the state. "That was true in the year 1250. But did you know that by 1300, the city had been almost entirely abandoned? To this day, no one knows why it happened so quickly — or why it happened *at all*." The adults all murmured and nodded. Kirsten preened. I slipped out the back.

Maybe I could track down Caleb and Dillie. Running around with them *had* to be more interesting than this, even if they did insist on calling me Lizard.

"Hey, what's your hurry?"

I stopped short. Jake was leaning against the

back of the Interpretive Center, chucking stones at a huge CAHOKIA MOUNDS sign. It was about six feet wide, with a painting of a giant green lump at its center. "Well?" he asked when I didn't say anything. "Where are you going?"

"Oh. Uh, nowhere." *Think*, I told myself desperately. I had to come up with something fascinating to say before he stuck his earbuds in again. But my mind was totally, pathetically blank.

"Too bad. Figured you might know something I didn't."

"What do you mean?" I asked. Immediately, I wished I hadn't. I didn't want him to think I was some dumb little kid who couldn't understand him.

But he just tipped his head back and gave me a slow, wide grin. It was the first time I'd seen him smile. "I was hoping you'd found something interesting for us to do."

Us? We were an *us*?

"Yeah, it's totally boring here," I said. *Casual*, I told myself. *Think casual.*

Jake didn't answer. Instead, he scooped up a few more rocks and started throwing them at the sign again. The stones clanged off the metal.

Ping!

Ping!

Ping!

"You're really good at that," I said.

He looked at me like I was crazy. "It's a big sign," he pointed out. "It'd be hard to miss."

"No, I meant . . ." What I meant was that he hit the same place on the sign each time, like he was pitching a baseball. I wanted to ask if he played baseball, and if that's why he was always listening to games. But if I did that, he'd probably ask me if I liked baseball, and I would have to admit that I was totally clueless. Then he might decide we had nothing in common.

Long seconds passed. Jake didn't tell me to go away — maybe because he'd forgotten I was there. Finally, I couldn't take it anymore. "Anyway, I'm just going to go —"

"You want to try?" he said suddenly. He held out his hand, palm up. There was a rock sitting in the center. "Go for it," he said. "It feels good."

I scooped up the rock and flung it at the sign as hard as I could, pretending it was my parents' road atlas.

Ping!

It did feel good.

"So, how come they call you Lizard, anyway?"

Jake asked, as I started collecting a handful of rocks.

"No one calls me Lizard," I said quickly.

"Sure they do," he said. "Caleb. Dillie. I've heard them. It's, like, your nickname."

I could feel the heat rising in my cheeks. "No, it's not," I said furiously. "It's just some stupid thing they —"

"I think it's cool," he said.

I froze.

No one had ever called me cool before. Except for Sam and Mina, and they *had* to think I was cool. It was in the best friend rule book. But no one else did. Especially not incredibly cute baseball-playing ninth graders.

"Lizard," he said slowly. "Yeah, I like it. Zard. That's what I'll call you. That cool with you?"

"Yeah," I said.

Okay, maybe I didn't *say* it. Maybe I *squeaked* it. He'd made up a name for me. Like a secret, just between us.

"Yeah, that's cool with me." I lobbed another rock at the sign, slamming it straight into the bright green mound at its center.

Ping!

* * *

Location: Granite City, Illinois
Population: 31,301 in Granite City, 13 in the Ramble Rose Motel, 6 miles out of town
Miles Driven: 673
Days of Torment: 9

The Ramble Rose Motel looked pretty much like all the other motels we'd stayed in so far. A dingy one-story red building curved around an empty parking lot. Each room was named after one of the states on Route 66. My parents got Texas, Caleb and Jake got Arizona, and Dillie, Kirsten, and I ended up in New Mexico. But as far as I could tell, there wasn't anything particularly New Mexico about the room, other than the cactus painting hanging over each twin bed — and the fact that it was really, really hot.

When they were trying to sell me on this trip, my parents forgot to mention that *real* America wasn't air-conditioned.

As soon as we dumped our bags, Dillie scrambled up on one of the beds.

"Dillie, no jumping," Kirsten snapped. It was like this every night. *No jumping on the beds. No candy. No TV after nine. No exploring after curfew. No whispering after lights-out.* It was the first time in my life I'd ever stayed in a hotel room without my mom and dad. If Sam and Mina were around, we'd be having the greatest sleepover in the history of sleepovers. I'd be having *fun*. Instead, I was stuck with Kirsten — and Kirsten didn't believe in fun.

It was seriously unfair. Big sisters were supposed to be cool. Okay, maybe not when they belonged to you, but *other people's* big sisters were supposed to be cool. Other people's big sisters let you stay up late and eat nachos and cookie dough for dinner. They knew about makeup, when you should wear it and when you shouldn't, and how much of it made you look like a clown. They had advice about boys, like when to call them and when to let them call you, and what it meant if one of them had a whole seven-minute conversation with you and gave you a cool nickname and then never said another word to you for another 374 hours. (Not that I was counting.)

In some alternate, bizarro universe, there was probably a bizarro Kirsten who was totally awesome. Bizarro Kirsten gave bizarro Dillie and bizarro Liza awesome makeovers and awesome advice and let them stay up after hours eating awesome snacks and watching awesome late-night TV. But in *this* universe, Kirsten was a total dud.

That night, a few minutes after we dropped our

bags in the corner, Kirsten's cell phone buzzed. "Finally!" she squealed, snatching the phone out of her pocket and pressing it to her ear. "Hello? Where have you —? I mean, hey. What's up?"

"Tell him how much you miss him," Dillie said, batting her eyelashes at Kirsten. "Tell him how much you looooooooove him."

"Shhhh!" Kirsten hurled a pillow at her sister.

"Oh, Thomas!" Dillie squealed. "Kirsten loves you sooooo much!"

Kirsten's eyes bugged out. "Thomas, can you hold on a minute?" she asked sweetly. Then she slapped a hand over the mouthpiece of the phone. "Delia Morgan Novak, shut your mouth. *Right. Now.*"

"Who do you think you are?" Dillie shot back. "Mom?"

"I can *get* Mom," Kirsten warned.

"And tell her what? That I'm bugging you while you're on the phone with your secret boyfriend? The one you're not even supposed to have?"

I looked up at Kirsten, surprised. She didn't seem like the type to have a secret boyfriend. That would be against the rules.

Kirsten just sighed, sounding disgusted. "I'm going to take this call *outside*," she said, glaring at Dillie.

"But Kirsten, we're not supposed to leave the room," Dillie said sweetly. "And you're definitely not supposed to leave us in here by ourselves. What if we get into trouble? I wouldn't want to get *you* in trouble."

Kirsten narrowed her eyes. "Okay, what do you want?"

"We stay up as late as we want," Dillie said firmly. "And you bring us back some snacks from the vending machine. Chips, a Snickers bar, and —" She glanced at me. "What'll it be, Lizard?"

On the one hand, I wasn't sure I wanted to team up with Dillie. On the other hand . . . I was hungry. "Anything chocolate," I said, futzing with my camera so I wouldn't have to look at Kirsten. "Um, please."

Kirsten just muttered something about blackmail and slipped out the door, slamming it behind her. Dillie flopped back on the bed and kicked her legs in the air. "Free at last!" she cried. Then she jumped to her feet. "So now what?"

"What what?"

"She'll be out there on the phone with *Thomas*" — Dillie fluttered her eyes and raised her voice an octave as she said the name — "for at least an hour. What should we do?"

I shrugged.

So we did everything. Well, everything you can do when you're trapped in a 16-by-16-foot motel room in the middle of nowhere. We jumped on the sagging beds, competing to see who could jump highest and slap the ceiling. We tapped Morse code messages on the walls — then freaked out and screamed when someone tapped back. We raided the mini-fridge for a guaranteed sugar rush — but chickened out at the last minute when we saw the sign with prices like SNICKERS BAR: $7.

Instead, we decided to mix up our own concoction. After all, motels may charge you seven dollars for candy, but they give you plenty of other stuff for free. Stuff like shampoo. Moisturizer. Mouthwash. Hand sanitizer. Conditioner. Toothpaste. A cornucopia of mini bottles that, when mixed together, turned into a thick, foul-smelling, greenish brown goo.

"Now try some on your hair," Dillie said.

"Are you insane?" I eyed the goo. "*You* try it."

Dillie hesitated for a moment; then her eyes lit up. "Better idea."

I watched, half in horror and half in awe, as she squeezed Kirsten's special bottle of shampoo into the sink . . . and replaced its contents with our own special mixture.

"I just want it on the record that I wasn't involved in this," I said, backing away.

Dillie raised her eyebrows. "Bet you wish you were."

Maybe.

We pawed through all the drawers and closets, hunting for whatever weird stuff previous guests might have left behind. We found: One left sock, brown, with a hole by the big toe. Three buttons of assorted colors. One gigantic ball of lint. One fuzzy breath mint. Two pens with PANKOW TRUCKING: BARGAIN RATE, NEVER LATE, ALWAYS GREAT etched across them in pale green. And, under the dresser, one freakishly big dead cockroach.

"Ahhhhhh!" I jumped up onto the bed, trying not to imagine what might be crawling around beneath the covers.

Dillie backed away, very slowly. "It's just a . . . bug," she said, sounding unconvinced. "A big . . . big . . . big . . ." She shuddered and jumped onto her bed. "Maybe we should forget we ever saw that."

"Deal."

To distract ourselves, we flipped on the TV. There was nothing on but a three-minute loop of "Welcome to the Ramble Rose Motel" and a woman who had her own fitness show, *Candy's Cooking*

Calisthenics! (She exercised while she baked, then rewarded herself by chowing down on chocolate cake fresh out of the oven.)

Bored, or maybe still trying not to think about potential creepy crawlies beneath our beds, Dillie grabbed my camera and started fiddling around with it. She peered at me through the viewfinder.

"Careful!" I warned her. The camera might have been old and annoyingly non-digital, but it was still my most valuable possession.

"So how come you always take such boring pictures?" Dillie asked.

"I do not!" Like it was my fault there was nothing interesting to take pictures of.

"You do, too," Dillie said, pretending to snap pictures of various parts of the room. "Ooh, a highway. Click. A mound of dirt. Click. A giant catsup bottle. Click. Bo-ring."

"Can I help it if this whole trip is boring?" I snapped. "What am I supposed to be taking pictures of?" I would never admit it to her, but even back home, I never had an answer for that one. I didn't really know why I wanted to take pictures in the first place. I just liked having the camera in my hands — I liked the idea of freezing a moment in time and keeping it around forever. But that didn't make it any easier to choose *which* moment to freeze. What kind of photographer can't come up with anything good to photograph?

The boring kind.

"*Real* stuff," Dillie said. "Like, how about that guy at the diner tonight who kept sticking his finger up his nose when he thought no one was looking? Now, *that's* a picture."

"Gross!" I swallowed a laugh. What was this obsession that everyone had with being *real*? If my parents weren't so into finding *real* America, we wouldn't be on this trip in the first place. We'd be in a hotel on the beach somewhere, ordering room service and eating at chain restaurants and going to the movies and doing all the stuff my parents refused to do. Or maybe we'd just be home. That was *real*, wasn't it? Why did getting *real* have to mean driving halfway across the country and having dinner next to a nose-picker?

Dillie held the camera at arm's length and turned the lens toward herself, then stuck out her tongue.

"Don't, you'll waste —"

The flash went off.

"— film."

Dillie pounced on my bed and shoved the camera in my face. "Come on, do something interesting," she urged me. "Let's make a memory!"

I snatched the camera out of her hands. "Make a memory with your own camera," I muttered. *If only Sam and Mina were here*, I thought. *They'd never tell me I was boring.*

That's when I had my brilliant idea.

Maybe I couldn't bring them on the trip with me — but I could still bring the trip to *them*. I would document every horror, every humiliation, every weird, freakish, annoying, or insanely boring thing that happened. And then I would make a souvenir scrapbook for each of my best friends. *Liza's Photojournal of Route 66.*

No — more like: *Liza's Photojournal of Misery and Torment.*

I handed the camera back to Dillie. "You know what, Dillie? You're right," I told her as she started making wacky faces into the lens.

"You mean it?" she asked. "No more boring pictures of scenery and stuff?"

I grinned, already drafting some captions. *Real "fun" in the real middle of nowhere with my really strange roommate.* "I mean it," I told her. "Go for it. Let's get real."

Chapter Three

Location: Missouri . . . Missouri . . . more Missouri . . . Florida — no, just kidding — *still Missouri*
Population: 5,911,605 residents; 0 friends
Miles Driven: Enough to make me carsick — twice
Days of Torment: Too many

Supposedly, a person can get used to anything. Here's what I had to get used to: waking up first thing in the morning, also known as *earlier than I normally had to wake up for school . . . even though it was summer vacation.* Eating soggy bagels and stale cereal in the motel lobby. Jumping into the car with my parents and begging them to pop in a

CD or an audiobook or anything but the local radio station that I *knew* they would insist on. Losing the argument.

Then we would drive.

Sometimes, we would drive for an hour. Sometimes, we would drive for six hours. We always started out together, all three cars bunched in a tight herd, but then someone would stop for gas and someone else would stop at a scenic overlook and pretty soon our little red Volvo would be all alone on the highway. Not long after that, we would usually be lost.

Route 66 was pretty easy to follow, but the *real* America that my parents wanted to see — all the farms and basement museums and rusty bridges — those were the kinds of things you had to hunt for. Lots of twisty dirt roads, unmarked turns, signs for streets that didn't exist anymore, maps that apparently someone just made up from her imagination since they didn't have anything to do with the real world.

"I told you to turn right!" That was my dad, realizing we were going the wrong way — and that we'd probably been going the wrong way for an hour.

"You said left!" That was my mom, gripping the wheel, smiling that don't-mess-with-me death smile she flashes when she pretends she's not mad.

"Left, but then a *right* at the farmer's market," my dad clarified.

"We didn't *pass* a farmer's market."

"What about that fruit stand?"

"That was a man with a wagon of apples. You're telling me your directions say 'turn at the man with the apple wagon'? You're telling me that every day, all day, that man stands there with his apple wagon so that people like us will know where to turn?"

"All I'm *telling* you is that you should have made a right."

"No, you're telling me that you got us lost, aren't you?"

My parents almost never fought . . . unless they were trapped in a car together. Yet another reason that a summer-long family road trip was an *awesome* idea.

Every once in a while, between long car rides during the day and lumpy motel beds at night, there was sightseeing. A miniature Stonehenge. An old bridge that you could use to walk across the Mississippi River. And the Mississippi itself, which was kind of cool, except that the water was almost brown and had a bunch of bottles and food wrappers and an old sneaker floating down it. Oh well.

Other than car time, the other families were always around. *Always.* Dillie was always there, very excited and very loud and very weird. Caleb was always there, telling me that a word didn't mean what I thought it meant or that a sign reminded him of some book he'd read about something no one had ever heard of, or just clearing his throat with that little nervous cough that meant he had something to say but wasn't sure anyone wanted to hear it. (We usually didn't.) Kirsten was always there, pretending she was better than us.

And Jake was always there, too. Slouching in the background with his earbuds in, listening to a baseball game, pretending he was somewhere else.

Looking massively, brain-hurtingly cute.

We had so much in common. Well, we had one thing in common, at least: Both of us wanted to escape. Once he figured that out, we could team up. It was just a matter of time.

So that's another thing I had to get used to on this trip: waiting.

* * *

Location: Ash Grove, Missouri
Population: 1,430
Miles Driven: 899
Days of Torment: 21

"All right, everyone, time for an official announcement," my father said, trying to make himself heard over the noise of Auntie Horvath's Family Dinner Palace. When that didn't work, he stood up and clinked his spoon against his glass. "It's announcement time," he said.

It was our seventh diner dinner in a row, and I was getting a little tired of instant mashed potatoes and chicken pot pie. As usual, the adults talked to each other, droning on about whatever sight we were going to see the next day. Kirsten played with her phone, waiting for Thomas to call. Dillie and Caleb sculpted mashed potato fortresses and made bets about how high they could build their green bean towers. And Jake stared into space, while I watched him out of the corner of my eye, half hoping he wouldn't notice — and half hoping he would.

"Quiet, everyone!" Professor Kaplan boomed. That did it. Everyone at our table turned to stare. So did the rest of the restaurant.

Great.

My dad smiled at the group. "As you know, we came on this trip hoping to see the *real* America."

I swallowed a sigh.

"And so far, so good," he continued. "I think you'll all agree, this has been an eye-opening experience."

Jake glanced at me and smirked, then stretched his eye wide-open between his thumb and index finger. I burst into laughter.

"Yes? Liza?" My father raised his eyebrows.

I turned the laughter into a coughing fit.

"As I was saying." My father cleared his throat. "During the day, we're doing a great job of seeing the countryside. But at night, we just go into our rooms and watch TV — same as we'd do at home. What's real about that?"

"Well, if it's what we do, then isn't it real by definition?" Caleb asked quietly. Unlike Jake, he was trying to be helpful.

But that didn't keep me from needing to stage another fake coughing fit. This time, Dillie joined in.

"We've decided to change things up a little," my father said. "So after dinner, we're going to have some live entertainment."

"Are we going to the theater?" Kirsten asked. "I just love the theater."

"In a way," my father said. "Only better. We're going to be our *own* theater."

I swallowed hard. "Like . . . karaoke?" I asked, feeling the chicken pot pie churning in my stomach.

But my father didn't seem to notice my I'm-going-to-be-sick look.

"Excellent idea!" he said. "That's exactly the kind of creativity that's going to make this work."

"That's not really what I —"

"Family Entertainment Hour," he said proudly. "We're going to split into groups, and each group will be assigned one night of the week, Monday through Friday. On your night, you'll be responsible for providing live entertainment for everyone else."

"Don't forget the best part!" my mother prodded him.

"It gets better?" Jake muttered.

"That's right," my father said. "There's just one rule: The entertainment has to be tied into our location."

"Doesn't that sound like fun?" my mother asked. "Just a little extra challenge."

The other adults nodded enthusiastically.

"I think it sounds great," Kirsten said in a flat voice. Even the queen of sucking up couldn't manage a happy face. We were in trouble.

I just didn't know how *much* trouble.

My parents — who I *knew* were the masterminds behind this whole thing — assigned us to our groups. Professor Novak and Professor Kaplan. Mr. and Mrs. Schweber. The "kids" — which included me, Dillie, and Caleb. It apparently did *not* include Kirsten and Jake, who got to be in a group of their own. And the final pairing, my parents, who volunteered to provide the first night of entertainment, "to show you all how it's done!"

I wanted to disappear.

Dinky as it was, the Eastern Grand Motel had a small room next to the lobby where they served continental breakfast. In the morning, it would be filled with rubbery bagels, stale doughnuts, and a few bleary-eyed truckers eager to hit the road. But that night, it was all ours. My parents sweet-talked the night manager into letting us use it for Family Entertainment Hour. Which meant that at eight P.M. sharp, we sat cross-legged on the floor, waiting for my parents to put on a show. It also meant that anyone wandering by could join the audience. By the time my parents were ready to start, there were two truckers, three guys decked out in motorcycle gear, and an exhausted-looking family with three toddlers.

My parents burst out from behind the "curtain" (utility closet) and skipped out onto the "stage" (the square of floor not filled with truckers, bikers, and one very embarrassed daughter).

My mouth dropped open. They were wearing top hats.

"Branson, Missouri, the Live Music Show Capital of the World, is fifty miles south of here," my father boomed. "But who needs Branson when you've got all the live entertainment you could want right here?"

"So, in honor of the Live Music Show Capital of the World," my mother continued, "and to inaugurate a special tradition for a very special group of travelers, we present to you . . ."

"The Gold Family Showtime Revue!" they cried together.

Dillie sucked down a giggle. Caleb went even paler than usual. I just groaned and tried to pretend I was somewhere else.

My parents launched into some incredibly cheesy song about a man slaying a dragon for his lady love, and a woman drinking poison for hers — and at this point, I realized things were even worse than I thought. My parents weren't just prancing around in homemade costumes, singing corny show tunes. They were prancing around in homemade costumes, singing corny *love songs*. Thirty seconds into the dragon song, they switched gears to some song I sort of recognized about finding a time and place for their beautiful love.

Vomit.

I took a few pictures, figuring they'd make the perfect addition to the *Journal of Torment*. Complete with caption: *These people are not related to me. I swear.*

The nightmare dragged on and on and on. My parents gazed into each other's eyes. They flipped their top hats and pretended they knew how to tap dance. They sang ridiculous lyrics in loud, off-key voices. Song after song after song.

And then, the grand finale: "Oh, give me one last kiss . . ."

Oh, give me a break, I thought, and slapped my hands over my eyes.

When I pulled them away, my parents were still kissing.

There was a long pause, and then a few people started to clap. Very slowly. "That was great, Mr. and Mrs. Gold," Kirsten said limply.

My parents joined hands and took a deep bow.

"You'll get your chance soon enough," my father promised Kirsten. "You all will."

I could hardly wait.

"You asleep?"

I opened my eyes. Dillie's face was about an inch from mine. Yikes. "Not anymore." I yawned.

"Shhh!" She jerked her head at Kirsten, who was sound asleep. "You don't want to wake her up."

"No, I don't want you to wake *me* up," I corrected her. But I did it in a whisper. "What's going on?"

Dillie tugged me out of bed. "What's going on is that we're going swimming."

"Huh? It's the middle of the night," I said. "And the motel doesn't even have a pool."

"*This* motel doesn't have a pool," Dillie agreed. "But the one next door totally does. Grab your suit — let's go."

I checked the clock. It was past midnight. Under normal circumstances, I would have ignored Dillie, rolled over, and gone back to sleep. But my parents had just spent the night dancing and singing in plastic top hats — and they'd made it very clear that pretty soon I'd have to do the same thing.

These were not normal circumstances.

I climbed out of bed and stumbled through the dark room, fumbling to find my bathing suit. We changed and made it safely outside, where Caleb was waiting for us. I glanced at Dillie. "We couldn't go without him," she whispered. "It was his idea!"

"Really?" I asked, surprised.

"Well . . ." Dillie grinned. "He did say he wanted to go swimming. I'm just the one who figured out the where, when, and how."

"You sure we're not going to get caught?" Caleb said nervously.

"I'm sure it will be worth it," Dillie whispered, and led us into the dark, empty parking lot where our motel butted up against the Deluxe Motor Palace. A chain-link fence separated the two lots. It rose about five feet above our heads. "Come on," she urged us.

"What if it's electrified?" I asked.

"An electric fence? In a place like this?" Dillie laughed. "We're lucky the *rooms* have electricity. Besides, it's probably illegal to have an electric fence around a hotel."

Caleb cleared his throat. "Actually, as long as the owners comply with minimum safety standards, it's perfectly legal to —"

Dillie tied her towel around her waist and scampered up the fence, her hands flying along the chain links. "I'm not electrocuted!" she called down to us, a little too loud for my liking. "You coming?"

Caleb looked at me. His face glowed orange under the parking lot's fluorescent lights. "I will if you will," he said.

"Well . . . we've come this far," I conceded. With that, we climbed side by side, dragging ourselves up to the top. There was no electric shock, no barbed wire. We scrambled over the edge and climbed down the other side. The pool awaited.

If you could call it a pool.

"We snuck out for *this*?" I asked. Yes, it was a cement cube filled with water. And yes, it was surrounded by familiar NO RUNNING! and NO DIVING! signs. But that didn't make it a pool. More like a *cess*pool.

"Have a little vision," Dillie said. "Think of this as our tropical oasis." She leaped into the air, curled her knees up to her chest, and cannonballed into the water with an enormous splash. "Feels great!"

Caleb ran toward the edge, but stopped just before plunging in. He dipped in a toe. "It's cold."

"Isn't that the point?" Dillie asked, backstroking across the pool.

It was an incredibly hot night. There was no breeze. I could feel the sweat trickling down my back. Caleb took a deep breath, pinched his nose between his thumb and forefinger, and jumped in. He surfaced with his hair plastered to his face. "She's right, Lizard," he said. "It feels great!"

"*Don't* call me Lizard," I growled. But I sat down on the edge and dipped my feet into the water. It was ice-cold — perfect.

"Maybe . . ." I murmured.

That's when Dillie surfaced beside me, grabbed my ankle, and pulled.

"Aaaaagh!" I shrieked. Bad idea. Water flooded my mouth. I burst to the surface, coughing and shivering. "You're going to pay for that!" I shouted, forgetting that we were supposed to be quiet. I splashed toward Dillie. She ducked underwater again. I chased after her — partly to get revenge, partly because swimming was warmer than staying still.

Dillie popped her head above water just long enough to shout, "Come and get me!" then took off for the other end of the pool. I chased her back and forth, always just a few arm lengths behind.

When I finally caught up, I was too tired to do anything but flip over onto my back and float.

The stars were diamond bright.

Dillie was squealing, Caleb was splashing, some kind of night bird was keening some kind of night song. But when I let my ears drop below the waterline, there was nothing but a rushing silence.

That lasted about forty-five seconds.

Then Dillie and Caleb launched a sneak attack, popping up from beneath me and tossing me halfway across the pool. After that, it was war.

But it turned out that splashing, swimming, pouncing, chasing, sputtering, dunking wars are the kind you can't actually win. "Truce!" I called, gasping for breath. I started inching closer to Dillie. If she bought the truce thing, it would give me the perfect chance for an ambush.

"You give up?" Dillie taunted, then struck first. She launched a tidal wave straight at me.

"Never!" I shouted, ducking under just in time. As soon as I surfaced, I launched another offensive in her direction. Dillie got clear; Caleb got doused.

"*I* give up!" he offered, spitting out a mouthful of water.

We ignored him.

"You'll never win," Dillie warned me.

"*You'll* never win," I shot back. I was a champion splasher.

Caleb moaned and sank beneath the water. "*I'll* never win," he whimpered, paddling toward the shallow end. It gave me an idea.

"Truce," I suggested again. But this time I meant it. I raised my arms high above the water, where they couldn't do any splashing harm. "I've got a better way to settle this. We race."

Caleb served as starter, judge, and referee. "Ready . . . Set . . . *Go*!" He karate-chopped his hands into the water and we took off. I swam as fast as I could. I imagined that the other side of the pool was New Jersey, and I was swimming home. Back to my house, back to my friends, back to the summer I was supposed to have. And when I slapped my hand against the far ledge, I was certain I'd won.

"Tie!" Caleb shouted. Dillie looked just as surprised as I did.

So we tried again.

I won the swim-without-moving-your-arms race, the swim-like-a-mermaid race, the who-can-swim-the-farthest-underwater race, and the dead man's float contest. Dillie won the swim-without-moving-your-legs race, the hopping-across-the-shallow-end race, the doggy-paddle race, and the who-can-hold-a-handstand-longer-without-falling-over contest. She also lasted longer than I did — ninety-eight seconds — sitting in the incredibly gross nearby hot tub with its lukewarm water and its suspicious smell.

For a tiebreaker, we decided to dive for objects on the bottom of the pool. We didn't have any coins or colored rods, so we tossed in our shoes. At least, Dillie and Caleb tossed in their shoes. I tossed in my flip-flops: They floated.

Dillie burst into laughter.

Caleb shook his head. "I wonder if it's some combination of their composition and surface area distribution. Huh."

I stared at him. Under any normal circumstances, that would have been a good time to explode with frustration. Dillie was laughing at me, Caleb was being a know-it-all. . . . It should have been annoying. It *was* annoying. But it was also two A.M., in some random motel pool that we weren't even allowed to be swimming in — and the soaking clumps of brown hair plastered to Caleb's face made him look like a soggy poodle.

What could I do but laugh?

And then the grin dropped off my face.

"Shhh!" I hissed. "You hear that? Someone's coming."

"Ha-ha," Dillie said. "Very funny."

"No!" Caleb whispered. He sank low in the water. "Look!" He pointed toward the hotel, where a flashlight beam was wobbling through the darkness.

"It must be a security guard," I moaned. "We are so busted." There was no way we could get out of the pool area in time. And even if we could, what were we supposed to do — run through the dark in our bathing suits, soaking wet, and somehow sneak back into our motel room without anyone noticing?

I wondered if cheap motel security guards came with attack dogs.

"Stay calm," Dillie ordered. "We'll think of something."

"My mom's going to kill me," Caleb muttered, sinking so low that the water lapped against his nose.

Footsteps approached the pool.

"Everybody hold your breath," Dillie commanded.

"What?" I asked, then felt her hand clamp around my wrist. I barely had time to suck in a deep lungful of air before she dragged me down under the water.

We sat at the bottom of the pool, eyes wide-open in the gross murky water, hair flowing like seaweed, cheeks puffed out with air.

Ten seconds passed.

Twenty.

Thirty.

Caleb broke first, blasting helplessly to the surface. Dillie shot up a moment later, air bubbles streaming from her mouth. I stayed down there until it felt like my lungs were going to explode. Finally, I couldn't take it anymore. I pushed off from the bottom of the pool and rocketed toward the surface. Water streamed down my face as I gasped for air. It had never felt so good to breathe.

For a moment I was aware of nothing but the rush of air into my lungs.

Then I noticed the laughter.

Caleb and Dillie were thrashing in the water, hysterical. And standing at the edge of the pool, flashlight in hand . . . that was no security guard.

That was Jake.

"You kids know that trespassing is against the law, don't you?" he said in a fake stern voice.

"Oh, please don't arrest us, sir," Dillie squealed, choking on her giggles. She splashed me. "Smile, Lizard. Jake's not going to tell on us, is he?"

Jake's smile was lit up by the flashlight. "Not on you, no. But maybe the twerp here," he added, kicking a wave of water toward Caleb.

Caleb ducked out of his way, grimacing. "Come on, Jake," he pleaded. "You tell my mom and she'll —"

Jake shook his head. "That kid just can't take a joke, can he, Zard?"

I loved it when he called me that — especially when it was too dark to see me blush.

"Don't worry," Jake said. "I won't tell on you. Any of you."

"In that case — want to come in?" Dillie asked. "Water's great."

I couldn't believe the way she was talking to him, like he was just a normal person.

He shook his head. "Not my thing. You kids have fun. Try not to drown." As he walked away, Caleb and Dillie burst into laughter again.

"I can't believe we thought *Jake* was a security guard," Dillie giggled. "And look at you, Caleb, you're *still* scared of getting in trouble."

"Well, *I* can't believe your brilliant plan was to hide at the bottom of the pool," Caleb shot back.

"Hey, it could have worked," Dillie said. "Right, Lizard?" When I didn't answer, she dove underwater, kicking toward the other side of the pool. She resurfaced and waved at me. "Tag—*you're* it!"

But instead of chasing her, I swam to the edge of the pool and hoisted myself out. How was I supposed to just go back to splashing around like nothing had happened? Like Jake, of all people, hadn't seen me soaking wet, hair plastered all over my face, snot probably dripping from my nose? *You kids have fun*, he'd said. Like I was just some little kid playing a little kid game.

"Where are you going?" Dillie shouted as I wrapped a towel around myself.

"Back inside," I told her.

"You want us to come with you?" Caleb asked. "You shouldn't be walking around out here by yourself. It's dark."

"I'll be fine," I said. "You kids have fun."

Chapter Four

Location: Tranquility Lake Recreation Area, Oklahoma
Population: Too many RVs, too many tents, too many campers
Miles Driven: 1,237
Days of Torment: 25

Crossing the Oklahoma border meant three things:

1. We were safe from any more show tune-themed family entertainment hours. At least until we got farther west. I didn't even want to imagine what kind of show my parents

would decide to put on once we were in spitting distance of Las Vegas.

2. We'd seen all we would ever see of Kansas. Since the *Wizard of Oz* was my third favorite movie, I'd been secretly looking forward to this stretch of the trip. I didn't know that Route 66 only winds through Kansas for thirteen miles. We passed a power plant, a park, three old bridges, a general store, and suddenly we were in Oklahoma. No wizards, no twisters, no yellow brick road. Just plenty of grass. And some cows.
3. Camping time.

Our parents had lined up a steady stream of cheesy, grungy motels for us to stay in. But they were also determined to *connect with the land.*

Enjoy those wide-open spaces.

Commune with the — wait for it, the word that always spelled my doom — real *countryside.*

After three weeks of skeevy motels, I was almost looking forward to setting up my tent. Camping looked like fun in the movies. It seemed easy to ignore the whole sleeping-outside-in-the-mud thing. Even though you're lying there, trying to pretend that there aren't ants in your sleeping bag, you're staring up at a starry sky or out into a landscape of beautiful nothingness.

Except in real life, I found out, you're just staring out at a bunch of other tents. Instead of letting you spread out in the landscape of beautiful nothingness, the park authorities herd everyone into a big sandy parking lot. (Which was obviously how they managed to keep the beautiful nothingness a beautiful nothingness, but still — annoying.) It also turned out that in real life, the ants were the size of my thumbnail and were joined by buzzing flies the size of my fist.

In real life, birds didn't tweet beautiful melodies. They cawed and squawked and snatched the last bite of sandwich right out of my hand.

And in real life, you had to deal with campsite bathrooms. Enough said.

Not that there weren't good parts. Toasting grilled cheese sandwiches over the fire? Definitely good. S'mores tasted better in the wild than they did cooked over my stove top — even if I did manage to burn my first four marshmallows into black, bubbling gunk and almost light my hair on fire.

And then there was the smell. This whole part of the country smelled different than it did back home. My parents said the air was cleaner out here. I didn't really know what it would mean for air to smell “clean.” I did know that most motels smelled like detergent (if you were lucky), and that the inside of our car smelled like Cheetos and feet. But out in the park, it just smelled . . . empty. Crisp. Open.

But even a whiff of nature and the taste of chocolate-smothered marshmallows weren’t enough of a plus to balance out the most serious minus. It wasn’t the insects. It wasn’t the mud. It wasn’t even the bathrooms. It was Family Entertainment Hour.

And it was our turn.

“They’re going to love it,” Dillie whispered as we huddled in the tent with Caleb, preparing for our debut.

“I don’t care if they love it,” I shot back. “I just care that it’s over quickly.”

“Isn’t that the point?” Caleb reminded me.

It had been Dillie’s idea to do *The Wizard of Oz*, in honor of the five minutes we’d spent speeding through Kansas. But it was *my* idea to do *The Abridged Wizard of Oz*, the whole story start to finish in under five minutes. Since we’d gotten the five-minute version of Kansas, I figured we were entitled to the five-minute version of Family Entertainment Hour.

Even if our parents wouldn’t thank us, I was

pretty sure Kirsten and Jake would. They'd had their turn the night before, and they'd filled the time by reading aloud random lines from the newspaper and the back of a cereal box. According to Kirsten, it was a "Dadaist commentary on the commercialization of the media and the futility of trying to rationalize the randomness of modern life." Our parents totally bought it. But I was pretty sure it was just an excuse not to have to humiliate themselves with costumes and songs and barking.

Too bad we didn't think of that first.

I winced at the thought of Jake seeing me like this, with socks taped to the side of my head like floppy dog ears. I'd opted to play Toto and the flying monkeys, figuring that way I wouldn't have to talk. It didn't occur to me that instead I'd have to crawl around on all fours, bark, hoot, and generally make a fool of myself.

"Action!" Dillie cried.

We burst out of the tent. Our families were assembled in a semicircle on the ground, sitting cross-legged and waiting to be entertained.

We hadn't spent much more than five minutes putting together the show, but everything went as planned. At first.

DOROTHY (Dillie): Oh, here I am in Kansas, everything stinks.

AUNTIE EM AND UNCLE HENRY (Caleb): Do your chores!

DOROTHY: There *are* no chores somewhere over the rainbow. *Sigh.*

TOTO: Woof!

DOROTHY: Oh no, a tornado! I'm flying! Where am I now? And why are there tiny little legs with ruby slippers sticking out from under my porch?

WICKED WITCH (Caleb): My name is the Wicked Witch of the West. You killed my sister. Prepare to die.

TOTO: Woof!

You get the idea.

Later, Caleb played the Tin Man, the Scarecrow, *and* the Cowardly Lion, all at once: "I may be heartless and brainless and a big fat scaredy cat, but even *I* know that evil flying monkeys aren't a good sign."

That was my cue. I was supposed to start jumping up and down, flapping my wings, and hooting and hollering like an evil monkey — with half the campsite staring at me. With *Jake* staring at me.

"Monkey!" Dillie hissed. "Go!"

I closed my eyes, took a deep breath . . . and

started hooting and hollering and hopping. What choice did I have?

Family Entertainment Hour was supposed to be a little educational. Here's the lesson I learned: If you're going to bounce up and down and flap your arms around, don't do it with your eyes closed. Because you might go a *little* bit off course. You might slam into your costars, knocking all three of you to the ground . . . where you collide with a tent . . . which then collapses on your heads.

Show over.

No one stirred as I crept away from the campsite. I played the flashlight back and forth across the trail, keeping my eyes on the ground ahead of me. I wasn't going anywhere in particular. Just away.

The trail wound up a hill. I followed it to the top, then stopped, looking out at the night. The moon was almost full. A wide lake stretched out beneath me, moonlight gleaming on its glassy surface.

"Couldn't sleep either?" said a voice behind me.

I almost screamed.

Instead, I whirled around. Jake was grinning at me.

"You followed me?" I asked. Maybe it was because it was so late, or so dark, or I was just so tired, but I wasn't as nervous as usual. When someone has seen you hooting like a flying monkey, it's hard to worry about what they think of you anymore.

"I was supposed to let you just wander off by yourself?" he asked. "What if you got lost or something?"

"I'm not some dumb little kid," I said.

"Who said you were?"

Instead of answering, I sat down, curling my knees up to my chest. Below us, the lake was dotted with tiny lights. At first, I thought they were glowing fish — but then I realized they were reflections of the stars.

Jake sat down next to me. "They treat me like a dumb kid, too," he said suddenly.

I kept my eyes on the water. "Who does?" I asked.

"I don't know. My aunt and uncle. My parents. Everyone."

I figured he'd stop there, since that was about the maximum number of words he ever said in a row. But he didn't. "I'm not supposed to be here, you know that?" He ground a fist into the dirt. "I'm supposed to be at baseball camp. I'm shortstop. I told them I was letting the team down. I *told* them. But you know how it is."

I made some noise, like a half sigh, half hum, hoping he would see I *did* know how it was.

"It's not my fault they're splitting up," he said. "So how come I'm the one who gets punished?"

"Your parents sent you on this trip to punish you?" I asked, confused. Then his words actually sunk in. His parents were splitting up? Caleb had never said anything about that. Did he even know? Did anyone know, or had Jake just revealed a huge secret — to *me*?

He snorted. "They said it would be good for me. But they just wanted me out of the way so they could fight."

I didn't know what to say. "Sorry," was all I could come up with.

Totally lame.

"Whatever. So what about you?" he asked.

"What about me?"

I tried to come up with something that would make me sound interesting. But my parents weren't getting divorced, and I wasn't letting my team down. I was just boring old Liza Gold.

"It's obvious, every time I look at you," he said.

My face felt like it was on fire. "What's obvious?" I asked in a high, tight voice. Could he know what I was thinking? About *him*?

He laughed. "That you want to be somewhere else. Anywhere else."

I breathed a secret sigh of relief.

"So what is it?" he asked. "You leave a boyfriend behind or something?"

"Um . . ." Wasn't it pretty clear that I'd *never* had a boyfriend, never even come close? Or maybe he was just making fun of me. "Not really," I said feebly.

"Figured," he said. "You're probably not the boyfriend type."

Great.

"Probably leave a string of broken hearts."

The laugh popped out before I could stop myself. "Right. That's me. Breaking hearts wherever I go."

"See? I knew it!"

Was he *flirting*? No one had ever flirted with me before, but I always figured I would know it if it happened.

Of course, I also always figured I would know how to flirt back.

Instead of trying to say something clever or funny or cool, I just told the truth. "I miss my friends," I said. "I had this whole summer planned out, and then . . ."

"Your parents come up with a different plan, and you don't get a vote," he said. "Yeah."

"Yeah."

"You want to go back to the campsite?" he asked.

"Not really," I said.

"Yeah." He leaned back and stretched his legs out in the grass. "Me neither."

So we didn't go back. We just sat there. Not talking, not even looking at each other. Staring out at the lake or up at the sky. Waiting for the sun to rise.

It was the most romantic moment of my entire life.

Chapter Five

Location: Flycatcher State Recreation Area, Oklahoma
Population: 3 idiots in the woods
Miles Driven: 1,425
Days of Torment: 26

Sometimes I think your brain only has room for a certain amount of stuff. Like when you accidentally memorize a bunch of song lyrics the night before a Spanish test. And suddenly the next day you can't remember how to conjugate the verb *to sing*, but you know each and every word of the newest Jonas Brothers' song. Even if you hate the Jonas Brothers. (*Especially* if you hate the Jonas Brothers.)

That's what happened to me after that night on the hill. My brain got full. Here were the things I didn't have space to think about:

- The fact that we were camping, *again*.
- The fact that it was so hot that by nine A.M. my clothes were already soaked with sweat.
- The fact that we hadn't been to the grocery store in two days, and all we had left to eat were peanut butter sandwiches and carrot sticks.
- The fact that our parents were forcing Caleb, Dillie, and me to go on an "energizing hike" even though none of us had any energy, or wanted any.

I couldn't think about any of that stuff, because my brain was all fizzy and full from the night before. Why worry about sweaty T-shirts and boring hikes when I could worry about Jake?

Fortunately, there was plenty of time for that on the hike, since it turned out "hiking" just meant "taking a long, boring walk through the woods."

I had my camera with me, as usual. I'd been hoping to get a shot of some exciting animals — buffalo or antelope or bears or whatever kind of creatures hung out in the Oklahoma woods. But the most we saw were a couple squirrels, and even they ran away when the flash went off. So I was left with a bunch of pictures of rocks, trees, and a couple brown smears. (*"Bo-ring,"* Dillie pronounced, and secretly I had to agree.) At least I got a shot of Dillie dangling upside down from a tree branch, pelting Caleb with red berries. Perfect for the *Journal of Torment*, which was filling up even faster than I'd expected. I already had the caption: *Here we see the strange creatures in their natural habitat. . . .*

After an hour of this, I was pretty much done with the hike. Unfortunately, there were still two more miles before the hike would be done with me.

"I didn't even know there *were* woods in Oklahoma," I complained as another branch whacked me in the face. "I thought it was just a lot of flat stuff. And dust."

"Oklahoma is one of only four states with more than ten ecological regions," Caleb said. "It has eleven, including mountains, wetlands, prairies, forests —"

"Okay, Wikipedia, enough," Dillie said. "We get the idea. How do you even *know* this stuff?"

Caleb shrugged. "I read it in the guidebook."

"And *remembered* it?" I could barely remember what state we'd been in the week before.

He shrugged again.

"That's so weird," Dillie said.

Caleb scowled. "Is not."

"No, good weird," Dillie explained. "Cool."

"There's no such thing as good weird," Caleb said seriously. "Weird can mean supernatural, or strange-looking, or unusual, eccentric, exotic, outlandish, but there's no definition that means cool. If you mean cool, you should say cool."

"Okay, first of all, don't think I didn't notice that you're not just a walking guidebook, you're a walking dictionary. We'll come back to that," Dillie said. "Second of all, you're crazy. Words can mean whatever you want them to mean."

Caleb shook his head. "If words could mean everything, they wouldn't mean anything. They'd just be sounds."

"They *are* just sounds!" Dillie slapped her hand on a nearby trunk. "Someone somewhere came up with the idea of calling this a tree. They could have called it a *flibber*. A forest of flibbers. A dark, deep wood of flibbers. I'm in the mood to climb a flibber and pick some apples off an apple flibber and —"

"Stop it!" Caleb's face was red. "Tell her, Lizard."

"What?" I didn't want to get involved.

"Tell her she's wrong."

"Oh . . . well, I don't know, Caleb. You *are* kind of weird," I teased.

"But weird in a good way, right?" Dillie encouraged me. "As in cool-different, cool-unusual. Who wants to be *usual*?"

"We are *not* arguing about my quantity and degree of weirdness!" Caleb said, so outraged in such a prim, proper, Caleb way, that I had to laugh.

"I'm just kidding," I said quickly.

"So who's right?" Caleb asked.

"Um, both of you?"

"Try again!" Dillie charged.

"Neither of you?"

Dillie made a low, growl-like noise. "Lizard . . ."

"Liza!" I corrected her. "Okay? You want to know who's wrong? You're wrong. You can't call a tree a flibber and you can't call me *Lizard*, just because you feel like it, or because you think I look all green and scaly or something."

"That's not why we call you Lizard," Caleb said. "It's because —"

A loud *CRACK* cut off the rest of his words.

We all looked up, wondering if a tree was about to fall on us.

"What was that?" Caleb asked very quietly.

I was afraid I knew.

Another deafening noise split the silence. This one was more of a *BOOM.* As if the sky was exploding. And then a moment later, it did.

Or, at least, the clouds exploded, right on top of us. Fat, heavy raindrops splattered on my head. The forest floor turned to mud.

"Come on!" I shouted over the noise of the storm. "Back to the campsite!"

We sloshed down the path, sinking deeper into the mud with each step. Wind howled through the trees. Thunder rumbled all around. Rain pummeled us. The fat drops had been replaced by tiny, hard hail-like pellets that drilled into us like needles.

"What's your rush?" cried Dillie as we broke out of the trees into a clearing. She stopped in her tracks, throwing her arms wide and turning her face to the sky. Her cheeks were streaked with water, and for a moment, I thought she was crying. But then I realized she was laughing.

There was nothing to laugh about — we were stranded in the middle of nowhere, drenched, probably about to be struck by lightning. On the other hand . . . a giggle burbled out of me. Maybe she was right. What *was* my rush? I was already as wet as a person could possibly be. My clothes were drenched, my shoes were filled with water, my hair was soaked. What was the point in running? The rain couldn't hurt me. And I counted five long seconds between the *FLASH!* and the *BOOM!*, which meant the lightning was still pretty far away.

I had to admit, it felt pretty good standing there with the storm raging all around. I tipped my head back, closed my eyes, and let the rain wash over me.

"Are you both insane?" Caleb shouted. Water streamed down his glasses as he frantically tried to wipe the mud from his jeans.

"Yes!" Dillie cried. She grabbed my hands and whirled me around in a circle. My feet skidded on the soft, slick grass lining the path, and I flew backward. Dillie's feet were all tangled with mine, and we toppled down together, landing on our backs in a puddle of mud.

We burst into giggles.

Caleb just shook his head. "You're both nuts," he said, trying to clear the water off his glasses.

Dillie climbed to her feet and slung a mud-spattered arm around him. "I know. That's why you love us," she said cheerfully.

Without thinking about it, I grabbed my camera and froze the moment. "Don't look now, but I think you've got a little mud on you, Caleb," I teased as thick glops of mud slithered down his shirt.

Caleb sighed, but he couldn't hide his smile. "Can we go back to the campsite now?"

We tromped slowly through the woods, sloshing and splashing in the mud. The pouring rain eventually faded to a drizzle, and as the sun came out again, our drenched clothes kept us cool. "Best hike ever," Dillie pronounced as our campsite finally appeared on the horizon. "Right, Lizard?"

I didn't say yes — but I couldn't say no.

"Don't call me Lizard."

* * *

Location: Hound Dog Hotel, Middle-of-Nowhere, Oklahoma
Population: The Schwebers, the Golds, the Kaplan-Novaks, and one bored, tattooed woman behind the front desk
Miles Driven: 1,442
Days of Torment: 26

I didn't get to talk to Jake all day. Not in the car with my parents, as we hurtled down the highway trying to stay ahead of the rain. Not at dinner in Mom's Café, where I was stuck at one end of the long table and he was at the other.

The longest conversation we had all day was ten seconds and four words long. It was after dinner, after we'd checked into the Hound Dog Hotel. Jake and Caleb's room was on the east side of the parking lot; ours was to the west. "Night, Zard," Jake said as he turned away from us.

If I had ESP, here's what I would have said to him, brain to brain: *Are you thinking about last night? Are you thinking about your parents getting divorced? If you want to talk about it, you can always talk to me. And also you look incredibly cute in that green sweatshirt. You should wear it all the time. I mean, not* all *the time, because then it would start to stink. But a lot.*

Here's what I said out loud: "Good night, Jake."

As we stepped into the motel room, Kirsten gave me a weird look. "So *that's* what's going on with you!"

"Something's going on with you?" Dillie asked.

"Nothing's going on with me," I said, throwing my bag down on one of the gilt-edged velvet chairs.

"You're going to claim you're not acting weird?" Kirsten asked.

Since when did Kirsten start paying attention to how I was acting?

"*Weird?* Look where we are," I pointed out. "The only thing weird is this room."

According to the sign hanging over the door, Elvis Presley, the King of Rock and Roll himself, had once stayed in this room. The owners had renamed the hotel in his honor and turned the room into a total Elvis shrine. (Once she'd heard about the room, Dillie had demanded it.) One wall was lined with album covers and fake solid gold records. The other was wall-to-wall photos and velvet portraits of Elvis: Young Elvis, Vegas Elvis, Fat Elvis, Soldier Elvis, even a hound dog dressed up like Elvis and propped against one of Elvis's guitars. The white hotel bathrobes were studded with rhinestones, just like Elvis's famous white jumpsuit. The pillows were shaped like hound dogs and broken hearts. The pay-per-view movies all starred Elvis, and the sign over the trash can read DON'T BE CRUEL — RECYCLE.

"Nice try," Kirsten said. "But you can't change the subject that easy. You've been acting weird all day. Like . . . *happy.*"

I wondered if her whole older-and-wiser act bugged Jake as much as it bugged me. I decided I'd have to ask him, next time we got to talk.

"See?" Kirsten said, triumph in her voice. She pointed at my face. "This is what I'm talking about. You're *smiling.*"

"Am not," I said.

"She's right," Dillie said, looking like she hated to agree with her sister. "You have been in kind of a good mood all day."

"So? What's weird about that?" I asked. "People can be in good moods without it being weird."

"*People*, maybe," Kirsten said. "You? No. You've been sulking for weeks, but then *Jake* tells you good night, and your whole face lights up like —" She laughed. "Like *that*!"

"Jake?" Dillie asked, now even more confused. "What does Jake have to do with any of it?"

"See?" Kirsten crowed. "She blushes every time you say his name."

"Do not!" I retorted.

"Jake Jake Jake Jake Jake Jake Jake," Dillie said, testing it out. The she nodded. "You're right, Kirs." She started laughing. "Really, Lizard? *Jake?* He's so . . ."

I turned my back on both of them.

"Obnoxious?" Kirsten suggested. "Boring?"

"You don't know him like I do," I said.

Then it occurred to me that I probably shouldn't have said that out loud.

"I knew it!" Kirsten said. She started talking in a high, fluttery voice. "Oh, Jake, you're so sweet and smart and misunderstood."

I threw a hound dog pillow at her head. Hard.

Kirsten sat down next to me on the bed. She smoothed out an imaginary lump in the bedspread (which was embroidered with a giant Elvis face, of course). "Look, I'm just saying that you should keep in mind that he's a lot older than you —"

"Two years," I said. "That's not a *lot.* A *lot* is, like, five or something."

"Just don't get your hopes up," Kirsten said.

I rolled my eyes. "Right. Because you know everything."

"I'm not saying I know everything —"

"You're *always* saying you know everything," Dillie put in.

"Fine!" Kirsten stood up and grabbed her cell phone. "You think I care if you want my advice? You're on your own. Good luck!" She stalked out of the room.

"Don't worry," Dillie said. "She'll be in a much better mood after she talks to *Thomas.*" She said it in the same lovey-dovey gushing voice she always used for his name. "So . . ." She bounced on the mattress. "You want to talk about Jake?"

"No."

Dillie shrugged and started poking around the room, the subject already forgotten. I didn't get it, the way things just rolled off her back. Little stuff made her so happy, and when it came to the big stuff, she just didn't seem to care.

As far as I was concerned, there *was* no little stuff. Everything you did and everything you said could be a big deal. Any word that popped out of your mouth could torpedo your cool factor in a heartbeat. If anyone knew the stuff that went through my head, they'd think I was a total freak.

At least, anyone back home would, I thought, looking around at the motel room. Out here, with all these different Elvises looking down from their gilded frames, you'd have to try really hard to look like a freak. In fact, out here it was starting to seem like the only truly freaky thing was being normal.

"Let's do makeovers," Dillie said suddenly.

"Really?" I was surprised. Makeovers were the kind of thing Sam and Mina and I did at sleepovers. We spent late nights haggling over nail polish colors and trying to decipher "Ten Steps to Glamour

Hair" in old magazines. It didn't seem like something Dillie would be into.

"Don't you want to?" Dillie said. "You could be *Jailhouse Rock* Elvis and I could be Vegas Elvis."

"Wait — what?"

"*You* want to be Vegas Elvis? Well . . . I guess that's okay."

"Dillie, I am *not* dressing up as Elvis."

"Why not?"

"Well, because it's . . ." Weird? Lame? Because playing dress-up was for little kids? "It just sounds boring."

"*You're* boring," Dillie muttered.

"You know what?" I said, sick of her calling me that. "Let's make a deal. You can give me an Elvis makeover — if I can give *you* a makeover. A different kind."

"What kind?"

"You'll find out. Deal?"

She scowled. "Fine, but we're starting with you." Then she skipped to the closet and pulled out one of the rhinestone-studded bathrobes. "And we're starting with *this*."

"What do you think?" Dillie asked as I did a slow turn in front of the mirror. The person in the mirror smiled when I smiled, nodded her head when I nodded mine, winked when I winked . . . but I still had a hard time believing it was me. Because what would *I* be doing in a white, rhinestone-studded bathrobe (the bottom half wrapped carefully around my legs to make it look like a jumpsuit), and Dillie's oversize black sunglasses? My dark brown hair was coated with enough hairspray to make it stand at least a foot above my head in a perfect pompadour. On my feet: Dillie's blue sneakers, the closest we could find to a pair of blue suede shoes.

"I think . . ." I laughed, then dropped my voice low and curled my lip in my best Elvis impersonation. "Don't be cruel, baby. You know I look like the king."

Dillie giggled. "The queen, maybe. But close enough."

"So what about *you*?" I asked, pushing her under the bathroom lights. "What do *you* think?"

Dillie took a careful look at herself. I'd washed her hair and then blown it out with a diffuser, giving her thick, blond waves. Her nails were coated with a plum-colored polish, and her skin was glowing after an orange blossom–scented face mask. A dab of pink gloss made her lips shine, and a little of Kirsten's eye shadow brought out the green in her eyes. I'd replaced the alien earrings and the saggy UFO sweatshirt with the cutest outfit I had in my suitcase: a flowy, hippie-style shirt that Mina had picked out for me, and cute denim capris.

"I think I look like Kirsten," Dillie said, not sounding very happy about it.

"You're way prettier than Kirsten," I said. It was true. I'd never noticed it before, but Dillie was pretty. And not just okay-pretty, like maybe I was on an especially good day. With her long blond hair, sparkling green eyes, perfectly pert nose, and pursed lips, Dillie was *really* pretty. The kind of pretty that would make a guy like Jake pay attention.

No. I am not jealous, I told myself. *I'm happy for Dillie that she looks so good. This is good news. I am a good person.*

And because it was something a good person would do, I told her again how great she looked. "You're beautiful, Dillie!"

She just shrugged. "But this isn't me," she said. "So it doesn't really count."

"It *is* you," I said. "It's just you with a few small . . . improvements. You could look great like this every day, if you didn't always dress so weird."

Oops.

The moment it popped out, I was sorry.

"You think I dress weird?" Dillie asked, sounding hurt.

"I thought . . . I guess I thought that was kind of the point," I told her. "You know. Weird in a good way. Like, cool."

Dillie dropped onto the bed. She was sitting on Elvis's nose. "Maybe it is. I don't know. I actually dressed like this for a while last year, like Kirsten. I thought it would make my mom happy."

"Did it?"

Dillie shook her head. "Turns out Professor Kaplan doesn't notice what I wear. I don't think she cares."

"Maybe you're lucky," I said, thinking about how I wasn't allowed to wear skirts more than an inch above my knee. My mom kept a measuring tape handy, and she wasn't afraid to use it.

"Yeah," Dillie said. "Maybe."

For weeks, I'd been gritting my teeth at Dillie's nonstop perky act, the way everything that happened was always "awesome!" and "fun!" and "no problem!" But now all I wanted to do was make her smile again.

"You do look great," I told her, steering her back toward the mirror. "I mean, not as great as *I* look . . ." I preened in my bathrobe and puffed up my pompadour. "But pretty good."

"You're right, I do," she said. "Although . . ." She scooped up her giant plastic green alien earrings and slipped them back into her ears. "Much better, don't you think?"

Weirdly enough, I did.

Chapter Six

Location: Silverado Ghost Town, Texas
Population: 0
Miles Driven: 1,649
Days of Torment: 35

Texas had fewer cowboys than I'd expected. What it did have were wide stretches of desert sand. Gutted towns with empty streets. Big men with big hats; big women with big hair. Big cities with big spaces between them. Almost everything about Texas, I quickly realized, was *big*.

Including the heat index. That's the thing that measures how hot it *feels*, rather than how hot it actually is. So say, for example, that the thermometer reads eighty-two degrees. But you're stuck in a car with a wonky air conditioner, and outside the sun is so hot you could fry some eggs on the street. And you don't care what the thermometer says; you're pretty sure that it's about 150 degrees.

That would be the heat index.

My point: Texas was hot.

For the first few days, I didn't notice. I was too busy trying to figure out what was going on with Jake. Did he like me? Did he *like* me? I kept track of everything he said to me — which wasn't hard, since he didn't say very much. There was the afternoon in Shamrock, Oklahoma, that he told me my tag was sticking out of my shirt. The dinner in Elk City, Oklahoma, when he bet me I couldn't balance a spoon on my nose longer than him. (I won.) And the time I almost fell on my face at the Texas Bug Farm (a field of half-buried Volkswagen Beetles). I caught myself just before I went splat, and he laughed. "Have a nice trip, Zard?" he'd said. "See you next fall."

Teasing, *plus* a special nickname. That had to mean something.

But what?

More than ever, I missed Sam and Mina. I needed some serious advice, and it wasn't the kind of advice I could get from Kirsten, Dillie, or anyone else on this side of the Mississippi. I was totally on my own.

After more than a week of obsessing over every little Jake-joke and Jake-smile and extremely adorable but confusing Jake-shrug, my mood was in the toilet. It was about then that I started noticing how hot it was.

Sweat-pouringly, T-shirt-drenchingly, blood-boilingly *Texas* hot.

It was the kind of day that any normal person would want to spend on the beach. Or safely inside, somewhere cool and air-conditioned. Our parents, on the other hand, deemed it the perfect day for a trip to the Silverado Ghost Town, an authentically re-created frontier land that would let us experience what life was like in the Wild West.

We'd passed by plenty of ghost towns on the way there. *Real* ghost towns, the kind that died when their mines went dry or their factories closed down or a new highway sent all the traffic in another direction. These towns weren't towns at all anymore. They were just clusters of empty buildings with boarded windows. Empty gas stations with cobwebbed pumps. And plenty of dust. Once, I thought I even saw a tumbleweed.

Silverado wasn't like that. More than anything,

the place reminded me of Colonial Williamsburg, this fake town my parents had dragged me to when I was nine. Colonial Williamsburg was supposed to take you back to the days of colonial America, and it was filled with people dressed like soldiers and fife players and Founding Fathers. All the stores were called things like "Ye Olde Local Shoppe" and "Dr. Johnson's Cheese and Apothecary," and the big highlight was audience participation in the butter churning. At Silverado, there were fake sheriffs and fake outlaws instead of fake patriots and fake redcoats. The stores were called things like "Rattlesnake Saloon" and "Ye Olde Blacksmithee." Instead of a butter-churning demo, there was a daily shoot-out in the town square. Which, I had to admit, was more interesting than the butter thing . . . but still just as fake.

That was the bad news. The good news was that for some reason, when Kirsten went off with the grown-ups, Jake stuck with us. (*You know the reason*, an eager little voice in my head said. *He's hanging around because he likes you.*) Well, technically he didn't stay *with* us. More like a few steps behind. He kept his earbuds in, and his head down. It was like we were all supposed to pretend that he was just a stranger who randomly ended up going to exactly the same places we did.

Not that you'd know it from the photographic record. Wherever I pointed my camera, Jake was careful to be somewhere else. I got an excellent shot of Caleb banging a gavel in the old courthouse, Dillie with her head and hands locked in stockades in the town square, and both of them behind bars in the old jailhouse. (This one was almost too perfect for the *Journal of Torment*. It clearly belonged on page one, with bold, black print underneath: *Help! I'm a prisoner of summer vacation!*). But the only picture I snagged of Jake was a shot of his back as he wandered into the gift shop.

"Dude, old-time baseball stuff!" he said as we stepped inside. "I didn't even know they *had* baseball back then."

"Actually, baseball as we now know it was popularized at the beginning of the twentieth century, just when this town was booming," Caleb explained. "And of course the game of baseball itself was —"

"Come on," Dillie said, dragging me over to a shelf filled with tacky souvenirs. "Unless you want to get stuck listening to them talk baseball all afternoon."

"Yeah, that would be . . ." I pictured me and Jake walking through the empty ghost town together. All afternoon. "Um, terrible."

"Talk about terrible." Dillie giggled as she began examining the merchandise. "I think this one's my favorite." She pointed to a shawl studded with bright pink sequins. "Or maybe this one." A giant gold brooch in the shape of a cactus.

"Definitely this," I said, showing her the matching cactus earrings. "Those would look absolutely perfect with my rhinestone cowboy boots." I stopped laughing abruptly, realizing that those earrings might actually be the kind of thing Dillie thought looked good.

But she was laughing even harder, and her nose was wrinkled in disgust.

Then she gasped. "Lizard, look! It's like they were made for you!"

"Don't call me —" The awfulness of what she was pointing at took my words away. "They" were two ceramic lizards . . . dressed up like cowboys. Their bright green skin clashed in a deliciously tacky way with their wide-brimmed purple hats and red cowboy vests. They were quite possibly the ugliest things I'd ever seen.

"What are you guys laughing at?" Caleb asked, popping up behind us. Even Jake — still trailing behind him — looked half interested.

Dillie and I exchanged a glance. Then I gave them my most mysterious smile. "Inside joke," I said. "You wouldn't understand."

"I feel like their little lizard eyes are watching us," Dillie murmured as we stepped out of the gift shop.

I giggled — but cut myself off as soon as I realized that *Jake's* eyes were on me. I didn't want him to think I was some silly little kid who just laughed at nothing all the time. I could talk about serious stuff, too. I could even talk about baseball. He just had to give me a chance.

Even better, I would make my *own* chance.

"Look!" I pointed at a sign on the ramshackle storefront we were passing. "Let's do it!"

"Take a ride through the old silver mines?" Jake read the sign in a dubious voice. "Sounds kind of . . ."

"Yeah, boring, I know," I said quickly, even though I thought it sounded a little bit cool. "But at least it's out of the sun."

A pretty girl with a blond ponytail and a Silverado employee vest waved us over. "Cool off in the silver mines," she said, beckoning us toward the entrance to the ride. "You know you want to."

Jake tilted his head. "I guess it could be cool."

I didn't like the way she was looking at him — and I *really* didn't like the way he was looking at her. But it wouldn't matter once we were squeezed into one of the little mine cars together. I didn't know too much about romance — okay, I didn't know *anything* about romance — but I was pretty sure that qualified.

"Come on!" Dillie said to me as she and Caleb climbed into one of the mining cars. "There's plenty of room."

"That's okay," I said. "I don't want to squeeze. Jake and I can just —"

"Don't be crazy, there's plenty of room!" Dillie patted the space next to her on the seat.

"I said, *that's okay*," I repeated through gritted teeth. I tried to send her a telepathic message: *Let it go*. Sam and Mina totally would have gotten my ESP. Of course, they wouldn't have needed it, because they wouldn't have tried to mess with my perfect plan in the first place. "Jake shouldn't have to ride all by himself."

"Why would he — *oh*." Dillie stopped, a slow grin creeping across her face. "Right. Sure, ride with Jake!"

But it was too late.

"No, go with your friends," chirped the blond girl. "I can ride with Jake so he doesn't get lonely."

I glared at her. "Don't you have to *work*?"

She gave me the fakest smile I'd ever seen. "It's cool," she said. "I won't tell my boss if you don't."

"But —"

"It's okay," Jake told me. "Go."

So I went.

I squeezed into the mine car next to Dillie, which was *not* big enough for three people. I folded my arms across my chest. I listened to the tinny voice piped through the car's speaker, droning on about how many pounds of silver the mine had turned out per year and how many miners had worked per shift and a million other details I didn't care about.

The ride seemed to last forever.

This would have given me forever to talk to Jake, was the kind of thing I was *not* thinking.

The mines were cold and damp and dark. They seemed like the kind of place giant spiders might like to play.

If I were sitting with Jake, he might put his arm around me and tell me not to be afraid, was the kind of thing I was *especially* not thinking.

The tinny voice was droning about the silver mining process and how we could try it out for ourselves at the pan-for-your-own-silver exhibit.

If Jake were here, I wouldn't be stuck listening to this ridiculously boring voice, because Jake would be talking about baseball. That would also be ridiculously boring, but it would be Jake talking in Jake's voice, and that would automatically make it interesting, was the kind of thinking that was slowly but surely driving me insane.

Finally, our car rolled through one last tunnel and emerged into the light. Dillie hopped out almost as soon as it stopped moving. "Let's go down to the Photo Parlor and take pictures of ourselves dressed up as cowboys," she said brightly.

"You go," I told her. "I'll wait here for Jake." I peered into the dark tunnel. If I could get Caleb and Dillie away before his car rolled out, we could at least have a *little* time together.

"We can wait," Dillie said as one empty mining car rolled out, then another. Where *was* he? "It's not like there's some kind of cowboy-costume emergency."

Caleb looked at me carefully. "Let's go," he told Dillie. "Liza can meet us there."

"You sure?" Dillie asked me. She looked at the empty mine cars rolling by, then back at me, like now *she* was the one trying to send some kind of ESP message. But whatever it was, I didn't want to hear it. I was on a mission.

"Go," I said firmly.

"Fine," she said. "We'll be at the Photo Parlor if you need us." And finally, they were gone.

I lounged against the side of the mine shack, waiting for Jake's car to show up. I didn't get why it was taking so long. Had I missed him? Maybe he didn't get on the ride in the first place?

And then he appeared.

He *and* the blond girl, side by side. Their hands glued together.

Their *faces* glued together.

I was going to puke.

"Oh!" the girl squeaked as the ride came to a stop and she spotted me. She pulled away from Jake and climbed out of the car. He followed her.

I just stood there. It felt like my foot was asleep. Actually, it felt like my whole body was asleep. That pins-and-needles tingling crawled across my skin. I was pretty sure my face was on fire.

Plus, there was the fact that I still really wanted to puke.

"Hey," Jake said, grinning like nothing had happened. Except that Jake *never* grinned. He always looked bored or cranky or sulky. I was supposed to be the only one who could make him smile. Me. Zard.

"I . . . I . . . uh . . ." I backed away. At least I didn't throw up on his shoes. "I have to go meet Dillie and Caleb. Later."

I spun and ran around the side of the building.

Then I stopped. I just needed to catch my breath. To think. To figure things out. I wasn't trying to listen — but I heard, anyway.

"So is she, like, a friend of yours or something?" the girl asked Jake.

There was a pause. Then, "Nah, just some little kid that's on this trip with us."

"It must be a total drag to be stuck with those kids all summer."

"Yeah."

That's when I finally forced my legs to start moving. But I only ran for a few feet before I realized I didn't have anywhere to go. So I just started walking. Staring at the ground. Trying to blink back the tears. Trying not to stomp and punch and scream and throw a temper tantrum like a "little kid."

I will not cry, I told myself. *No big deal. Why am I surprised?*

After all, he was two years older than me. He

was a baseball player. And I was just . . . boring, bland, *little* Liza Gold.

"Lizard!" someone shouted. Dillie darted out of a nearby building, waving her hands and running toward me. She was wearing a long, ruffled yellow skirt. Caleb followed, a wide-brimmed cowboy hat slipping down over his eyes. "Lizard, you have got to see these costumes," Dillie said breathlessly. "They're amazing, and we can wear whatever we want!"

"She's right, Lizard," Caleb said eagerly, tipping his hat. "It's great."

Lizard.

Such a dumb nickname. A dumb *little-kid* nickname. A nickname I had told them and *told them* and *TOLD THEM* not to call me.

"You okay, Lizard?" Dillie asked.

I lost it.

"No, I am not okay," I informed her. *"I am not okay!"*

"You don't have to shout," Dillie said.

"Yes I do!" I shouted, even louder. "Because you two will *not listen*! Can you hear me now?"

"Um, people are staring at us," Caleb said in a whisper.

"I don't care!" I yelled. And for the first time in my life, I really didn't. "Stop calling me Lizard! You know what? Stop calling me *anything*. Just *leave me alone*!"

This time when I ran away, I ran.

And I kept running.

I ran until I got to the very edge of the ghost town. I thought I would feel better once I was alone. I was wrong. Maybe it was because I was by myself on a hill that reminded me too much of that hill in Oklahoma and the night when Jake had finally seen me as an equal. Or so I'd thought.

Turned out he'd never seen me as anything but "some little kid."

Some little kid named *Lizard*.

I wiped my face angrily and pulled out my camera. For a second, I wanted to hurl it off the hill. Or bash it into a rock. It would be satisfying to see *something* break. But instead, I took a picture of the Texas desert stretching out beneath me. *Not quite happily ever after*, I captioned it in my head. But this one was too tormented for the *Journal of Torment*. It was just for me.

Footsteps crunched the ground behind me.

It's Jake, I thought. *He wants to apologize. And as soon as he looks at me, he'll realize that I'm the only one for him and we'll laugh about this whole thing and it will be part of the funny story of How We Met and —*

"You okay, Liza?"

It wasn't Jake.

I kept my back to Caleb. "Fine," I said, hoping he wouldn't notice that my voice was fuzzy. "So you can go."

He sat down.

"I don't want to talk," I told him, trying not to sound mean. Caleb wasn't the kind of guy you wanted to be mean to, no matter how rotten and twisted you felt.

He took off his glasses and rubbed the lenses against his shirt, trying to wipe off the desert grit. "You know why we call you Lizard?" he asked quietly. His eyes were really green and wide without the glasses. But then he put them back on, and I decided I liked him better that way. He looked more like Caleb.

"Because you love to annoy me?"

"Because you *asked* us to," he said.

That didn't make any sense.

"When we were seven," he continued. "It was on that trip to Florida. Our parents dragged us to some kind of alligator farm, and it was ridiculously boring until you started naming all the lizards and making up stories about what they were doing. You saved us from dying of boredom. And you made us call you the Lizard Queen for the rest of the trip."

I remembered the alligator farm, but not the rest of it. "That was a long time ago," I pointed out.

"Pretty memorable," Caleb said.

I didn't know what to say. I'd never really thought of myself as the kind of person that anyone remembered. If anything, I always figured I was easy to forget.

Caleb rummaged in his backpack and pulled out a small cardboard box. He shoved it in my direction. "These are for you," he muttered, his face bright red.

"You got me a *present*?"

"No," he said quickly. "I mean, yes, I guess, technically, but not really. It's just something — no big deal. I just . . ." He looked down. "I wanted to cheer you up."

I opened the box. Two porcelain figurines were nestled inside: the lizard cowboys Dillie and I had seen in the gift shop that afternoon. Specifically, the *ugliest* things we'd seen that afternoon. Or ever.

"Oh," I said, trying frantically to think of something else to say. "They're . . . wow."

"You like them, right?" he asked eagerly. "I saw you looking at them in the gift shop, and . . . I don't know, it seemed like they made you happy."

I realized I was smiling. "They really do, Caleb," I said honestly, slipping the box into my bag. "They're awesome."

And they were. Weird, tacky, and hideously, mesmerizingly ugly.

But awesome.

Dillie popped up behind us and flopped down in the dirt. "So what are we talking about? How much Lizard — I mean, Liza — hates us?"

"I don't hate you," I said.

"Really?" Caleb asked.

I gave him a light shove. "How could I hate the person who gave such awesome lizard cowboys to the Lizard Queen?"

Dillie burst into laughter. "So you *do* remember!" she exclaimed. "How great was that?"

"Not as great as that trip to Tiny Town, when she suckered us into sneaking into the restaurant diorama and pretending we were giants, there to crush all of the miniature hungry people," Caleb said.

"How about when she carried that cardboard Pikachu cutout all over Santa's Candy Castle, and kept telling people that her pet Pokémon was hungry?" Dillie sputtered through her laughter. "And then pretended to cry when they thought she was joking, so that they'd give her candy just to shut her up."

"But the best one was —" Caleb started.

"The Ben & Jerry's Factory!" they said together.

Dillie shook her head. "You got us into that off-limits tasting room. And then you actually convinced them to give us free pints of their new flavor!"

"How do you guys *remember* all this?" I asked. "It was forever ago."

Dillie looked at me like I was nuts. "Who forgets free ice cream? That was epic."

"Legendary," Caleb agreed.

It all sounded familiar — most of it, at least. But I had a hard time believing what they were saying. Had I really been the mastermind behind all those adventures? "It just doesn't sound like me," I said.

Caleb looked away.

"People change," Dillie said softly.

I knew exactly what they were thinking. The person in those stories didn't sound like me because it *wasn't* me, not anymore.

But maybe it could be.

Chapter Seven

Location: San Jon, New Mexico
Population: 306
Miles Driven: 1,834
Days of Torment: 42

"Caleb's in," Dillie whispered to me a few nights later while Kirsten was sequestered in the bathroom on the phone with *Thomas*. (Even in my head, I'd started saying his name the way Dillie said it, in a fluttery, lovesick voice: *Thoooooomas*.)

"In for what?"

"You know." Dillie wiggled her eyebrows, waiting for me to catch on. When I didn't, she rolled her eyes. "What else? Getting back at Jake the snake."

"Who said we were getting back at Jake?"

"You don't have to *say* it." Dillie rolled her eyes again, like I was being dense on purpose. "He messes with you, we mess with him. That's just how it works, right?"

"Caleb really wants to help?"

"Caleb's got his own reasons for wanting to get back at Jake," Dillie said. "I don't know if you've noticed, but the guy's a total jerk. He treats Caleb like he's some kind of giant, glasses-wearing mosquito. Trust me, we just need to work out a couple problems, and then we can totally do this."

"Do what, exactly?"

Dillie hesitated. "Well, that's where you come in. We need a plan."

"And you want *me* to come up with one?" Ever since the ghost town, Caleb and Dillie had been acting like Lizard the Mischief Mastermind was back. But I wasn't so sure about masterminding any mischief.

On the other hand . . .

"You already have an idea, don't you?" Dillie asked.

I couldn't help smiling.

"I knew it! Never cross the Lizard."

She let out a cackle, then slapped a hand over her mouth, her eyes darting toward the bathroom door. In low, urgent whispers, we made a plan.

* * *

Location: Tucumcari, New Mexico
Population: 5,989
Miles Driven: 1,901
Days of Torment: 45

We waited for another camping night. It took a few days, but the wait was worth it, because the Tucumcari Area Campground was perfect. Enough room to set up camp where no one else could see or hear you. Hiking trails that twisted and turned through winding ridges, framed by prickly cacti. A shallow, nearly dry creek. Just what we needed.

It was torture, waiting for the perfect time to unleash our plan. Especially since that night, it was the professors Kaplan and Novak's turn for Family Entertainment Hour. The last time around, Professor Novak had delivered a lecture on the dining habits of west Texan gophers. This time, Professor Kaplan gave us a talk about the nineteenth-century explorers of the Southwest, with special emphasis on the history and geology of nearby Tucumcari Mountain. Since Professor Kaplan was an English professor who specialized in French poetry from the 1600s, it wasn't clear to me how she'd managed to find so much heinously boring information about random explorers out here in the middle of nowhere.

As she droned on for one hour, then two, then finally paused for questions, I decided not to ask.

Finally, everyone crawled into their sleeping bags, zipped up their tents, and went to sleep. Everyone except me and Dillie, that is. We waited until midnight — and then we put our plan in motion.

"I heard something!" Dillie cried in a low voice, poking her head into Caleb and Jake's tent. I peeked in, too, trying not to laugh. Caleb, who was only pretending to be asleep, gave us a thumbs-up. But Jake didn't stir. Dillie repeated herself — louder this time, though still softly enough not to wake the grown-ups. Jake bolted out of his sleeping bag.

"Whaaaa?" he asked groggily, rubbing the sleep out of his eyes.

"Out there!" Dillie hissed. "A noise. What if it was a bear? Or, I don't know, a jackal?"

"Then you'll probably be safer in your own tent." Jake lay down again and shut his eyes.

Dillie glared at Caleb. He cleared his throat. "Uh, how can we help, Dillie?"

"We have to go see what it is," Dillie insisted. "All of us. It's safer that way."

"Good idea," Caleb said.

Dillie elbowed me in the side. "Yeah," I added. "Just to be safe."

Jake groaned. "I'm not getting any sleep until I do this, am I?"

"I would hate for you to get eaten by a bear," Dillie said sweetly.

Jake snorted, and mumbled something about how he'd rather take his chances. But he got up, switched on his flashlight, and led us into the dark.

"This way," Dillie said. We followed the path until it dead-ended in a dense growth of cacti. "Now," she whispered to me. "Go for it."

I hesitated, suddenly feeling a little guilty. Talking about getting revenge was one thing. Actually *doing* it . . . Did Jake really deserve that? I wasn't sure. But before I could say anything, Dillie screamed. "Skunk! It's a skunk!"

"What?" Caleb shouted, right on cue.

"Where?" Jake yelled, whirling around.

"I thought *I* was supposed to be the one to see the 'skunk,'" I whispered to Dillie.

She grinned. "That's what friends are for,

Lizard," she whispered back. "You can thank me later."

The whole scene was total chaos — Dillie and Caleb made sure of that. And when Jake's back was turned, Caleb slipped out a tiny water gun and shot him in the leg.

"What was that?" he yelped.

"What?" Caleb said innocently, slipping the water gun back into his pocket.

"I felt something. . . ." Jake's voice was filled with dread. "Wet. On my leg. You don't think it was . . ."

"Ugh, what's that smell?" Dillie asked.

Caleb faked a gag. "It's *Jake.*"

"I don't smell anything," Jake said.

"Well, of course not." Caleb did his best to sound like he knew what he was talking about, even though every word out of his mouth was a lie. "The person who gets sprayed doesn't smell it, not at first. There's a . . . an olfacto-depressing agent in the spray."

"Olfacto-depressing?" Jake echoed.

"That means it numbs your smell detector," Caleb said, taking several large steps away from Jake. "Consider yourself lucky."

Jake sniffed himself. "It's really that bad?"

Dillie started backing toward the campground. "If I don't get away from you, I'm going to puke."

I could have ended it at any point. But I kept my mouth shut.

"Wait!" Jake pleaded. "You have to help me! How can I get rid of the smell? Caleb, man, there must be a way. You know everything. Come on."

Caleb tapped his finger against his lips. "Well, you could take a bath in tomato juice."

Jake was getting more frantic by the minute. "I don't *have* tomato juice. Or a bathtub."

Caleb shrugged. "The smell should go away by itself. In a few weeks."

"A few *weeks*?"

"There may be one other way . . ." Caleb said slowly. I knew this was killing him. He hated it so much whenever anyone said anything that was incorrect or misleading. And here he was, spilling out one horribly wrong fact after another. "It's a traditional remedy, used for hundreds of years by people who didn't have doctors or tomato juice or anything, because they lived in the wild."

Jake nodded eagerly, jabbing a finger into his chest. "That's me! Stuck in the wild! Spill."

I pressed my hands over my nose and mouth

to keep in the giggles. (Hopefully it looked like I was trying to keep out the "stink.")

"Well, first you'd have to submerge yourself in fresh water, then cover yourself with earth, and let it seep into your skin for at least seven hours," Caleb said.

"That's it?" Jake asked. "Seems pretty easy."

"Seems pretty crazy," Dillie said, just like we'd planned. "You sure that will work?"

"Of course it will work!" Jake said. "This is Caleb we're talking about. Kid's a know-it-all freak. Only thing he's good for."

At the look on Caleb's face, I dropped the last of my doubts. Maybe Jake hadn't meant what he did to me. But he meant the things he said about Caleb, and that was enough. "Let's go," I said firmly. "We should get started, because you're really starting to *stink*."

Jake dipped a toe in the creek a few minutes later. "It's *freezing*," he complained. "You sure I —?"

"I'm sure," Caleb said.

Jake shuddered, but he waded into the ankle-deep water. "How am I supposed to 'submerge' myself when it's this shallow?"

"You're a smart guy," Dillie said. "You'll figure it out."

We lined up along the edge of the creek and watched Jake frantically trying to cover himself with the icy water. He cupped it in his hands and dumped it over his head. He drizzled water down his shirt and along his arms, shivering with cold. Finally, in disgust, he dropped to the ground and started rolling and splashing in the creek.

"This is just sad," Dillie said quietly, shaking her head.

"Sad?" Caleb repeated. "This is the greatest day of my life."

"And now we'll remember it forever," I said, pulling out my camera. Time to record Jake's humiliation for all time. "Say cheese," I murmured, hoping he'd be too distracted to notice the flash.

It was the most satisfying picture I'd ever taken.

Moments later, Jake stood up, soaking wet. "What now?"

Caleb pointed to the shore. "Now, you cover yourself with earth."

"You mean, like . . . dirt?"

Caleb nodded. "Head to toe. It'll leech out the skunk juice."

Jake came toward me. "Come on, Zard, smell me. Maybe the water washed out the stink."

I pinched my nostrils together. "Trust me, it didn't."

Jake sighed. But he did exactly as Caleb ordered him. He lay down and started rolling and flopping around like a fish. The dirt stuck to his wet skin and clothes, caking him in a thick layer of brown grime.

"That's probably enough," Dillie said. "Though I could watch this all night," she added under her breath.

"And I really have to sleep like this?" Jake asked.

"You don't have to sleep," Caleb said. "But you can't wash it off until morning."

Kirsten was waiting for us when we made it back to the campsite. She stood in front of our tent, glaring, and I was pretty sure we were sunk. Kirsten would wake our parents, tattle on us for wandering off, and Jake would find out the truth. But instead, she pursed her lips and pointed at Jake. *"You,"* she said. "You *stink*."

Dillie, Caleb, and I gaped at her in surprise.

"Skunk," Jake muttered. "I'm working on it."

"Well, work on it somewhere else," Kirsten ordered him. "Away from here."

"What?"

"You heard me," she said. "Get your sleeping

bag and take it far enough away that we can't smell you."

When Kirsten gave you an order, it was hard not to obey. Soaking wet and covered in mud, Jake slouched toward his tent, retrieved his sleeping bag, and dragged it about fifty feet away. He was still close enough that we could watch him toss and turn in his muddy pajamas.

"So, um, Kirsten," I said hesitantly. Even if Kirsten had somehow managed to figure out what we were doing, no *way* would she go along with it. "You really think Jake . . . *stinks*?"

"Definitely," she said. And then she winked.

* * *

Location: Somewhere between Tucumcari and Santa Rosa, New Mexico

Population: 3

Miles Driven: 1,924

Days of Torment: 46

Jake didn't tell on us. Not when he woke up to discover that the mud had hardened, turning him into a sun-baked mummy. Not when the grown-ups discovered him and wanted to know what in the world he'd been thinking. Not even when Professor Kaplan made it very clear that no one, nowhere, ever thought water and dirt would make a good remedy for skunk spray. Jake had just shrugged. "I don't smell anymore, right?" he said. "So something must have worked."

But from the way he looked at us, I knew that he knew.

Good.

After that, he didn't call me Zard anymore, and he didn't tease me, or bore me with his long baseball stories. He went back to treating me like he treated everyone else — like I didn't exist.

Even better.

After that, the days blended together, just like the dusty towns dotting the desert. Our cramped little Volvo was speeding along toward Santa Rosa and the Route 66 Auto Museum when the noise started. At first, it was just a small, quiet clanking, like the Ghost of Road Trips Past rattling its chains.

"What's that sound?" my mom asked, turning down the radio. She was navigating while my father drove. The Schwebers and the Kaplan-Novaks were already miles ahead, thanks to my parents' unscheduled, hour-long stop at the Route 66 Roadside Extravaganza! gift shop.

"It's nothing," my father said, cocking an ear to the side as if he could tell something from the noise. But my father could barely tell how to fill up the car when we stopped at a gas station.

The clanking got louder and turned into more of a squealing, grinding clatter, like someone had poured a jar of metal screws into our engine. That was when smoke started pouring out of the hood.

"I think we should stop, dear," my mother said in the voice she uses when she's trying not to completely freak out.

"You think?" My father, on the other hand, was using the voice that meant he was trying very hard not to break something. As he pulled over to the shoulder, the engine cut out completely. The car drifted to a stop about six feet past the shoulder, in the middle of the desert sand. A big, red, Volvo-shaped rock. We weren't going anywhere anytime soon.

"Everyone okay?" my mother asked.

"Everyone but the car," I pointed out.

"No one worry," my dad said. "We'll just take a look at the engine, and, uh, see if we can figure out what's wrong."

Well, we figured out where the engine was. We even figured out how to open the hood to *look* at the engine. It was still smoking.

"*Something's* wrong with it," my father pointed out.

"Very observant," my mother said.

They glared at each other. I held my breath, wondering which one would explode first.

But they both exploded at once . . . with laughter.

"I *told* you we should get the car checked out at the last gas station," my mother said, giggling.

"And I told *you* we should bring along that fixing cars for dummies book," my father said, leaning against the car, trying to get control of himself.

My mother patted his shoulder. "It's fixing cars for dummies, dear, not fixing cars for dummies who can't even fix themselves a sandwich."

After that, they were laughing too hard to speak.

I wondered how close the nearest mental institution was. And whether they had taxi service.

"Um, guys?" I said finally, sweating in the afternoon sun. The Volvo's air conditioner may have been wonky, but it was better than nothing. "What do we do now?"

"Don't worry, Liza," my mother said, drawing in a few deep breaths. "We'll just give the Kaplan-Novaks a call and . . . oh." She stared at her cell phone, brow furrowed. Then she started to laugh again.

"*Oh*, what?" I asked. "'Oh' doesn't sound good."

My father peered over her shoulder and chuckled. "*Oh*, there's no cell service out here in the middle of the desert."

"This is *not funny*!" I shouted. "We're stranded in the desert! With no car! No phone! No nothing! Why are we not *freaking out*?"

"No point in freaking out," my dad said. "This is just a minor setback. We'll get past it."

"How?" I demanded.

He smiled at me. It was his wicked smile, the one he used whenever I was foolish enough to complain about being bored and he suckered me into cleaning out the garage or alphabetizing his CD collection.

"Exactly like our brave and hardy ancestors would have," he said cheerfully. "We walk."

Chapter Eight

Location: The side of the road
Population: 3
Miles Walked: 2
Days of Torment: 46

We walked.

And walked.

"This is officially the worst family vacation *ever*," I said, about a million miles after we started out.

Okay, according to my mother's jogging pedometer, it was about a mile and a half. But when it's ninety degrees out, and there are no landmarks except for the cacti and a coyote staring at you like it's waiting for dinner, one mile might as well be a million. (True, the coyote might actually have been a jackrabbit, but you can never be too careful.)

"It can't be that bad," my mom said, passing me her bottle of water so I could down the last few drops. I have to admit: Moms are good like that.

"I *thought* it couldn't be that bad," I said. "And then our car broke down in the middle of nowhere."

"Seems like you're having a *little* fun on this trip," my father pointed out. "Or was that some other Liza Gold I saw cackling all through dinner last night?"

That was only because Dillie had molded her soggy French fries into a surprisingly good replica of her mother's face.

"And you didn't look especially miserable at the Cadillac Ranch, when you kids were running around the cars, screaming at each other," my mother added.

We were only running because Dillie had ambushed me and Caleb with a Super Soaker she'd picked up at the gift shop, and then ran away before we could get her back. But we caught up with her eventually, just in time to dump a bottle of ice water over her head.

Mmm, ice water . . .

I got so distracted by the thought of a cool, refreshing bottle of water — poured down my throat or over my head or, preferably, both — that I almost forgot what we were talking about.

"Maybe she just means she's miserable spending time with us," my mom said. "Her annoying, embarrassing, ridiculous parental figures."

"Couldn't be," my father said. "After all we've done for her! Fed her. Clothed her."

"Stranded her in the desert," my mother pointed out. "Dearest daughter, is there anything we can ever do to make you forgive us?"

I couldn't help it — I had to smile. It was impossible not to, when my parents got like this. "You could buy me a car when I turn sixteen," I suggested.

My father pressed a hand to my forehead. "We better get her back to civilization soon," he said. "I think she's getting delusional."

* * *

Location: Roseland, New Mexico
Population: 224
Miles Driven: 1,920 by car, 4 on foot
Days of Torment: 46

It was dark by the time we got to the nearest town. Fortunately, it was easy to find the local garage . . . because that was pretty much the entire town. One garage, one general store, and one diner.

The general store and the diner were closed.

"So there's nowhere to *eat*?" I asked as my father climbed into the tow truck. He had to show the tow truck driver where our car was. The driver leaned out the window, winking at me.

"Don't worry, little lady," he said. "You won't starve, I promise."

They drove off, leaving me and my mom alone with the driver's slobbering guard dog. A spiky collar and thick chain kept it safely on the other side of the garage, but its teeth looked sharp enough to chew through the chain if it got angry.

"She won't hurt you," the driver had said, before disappearing. "She's a sweetheart."

Sure. A sweetheart with four-inch fangs.

At least our cell phone worked again. My mom called the Kaplan-Novaks and the Schwebers, who were twenty miles away at the rendezvous point. They piled into their cars and joined us at the garage, right around the time the tow truck returned with our sad, broken car.

"Good news!" my father said as he hopped out of the truck.

"The car's fixed and we can get out of here?" I guessed.

The tow truck driver shook his head. He was a large man, towering over us with a thick salt-and-pepper beard and twinkling eyes. *A little like Santa Claus*, I thought. *Except in this case, Rudolph is a Red-Nosed Doberman.* "That radiator hose is toast," he said. "It'll be at least two days before I can install a replacement and get you folks on the road again." He smiled and clapped a hand on my father's back. "But you're all welcome back to my place for an old-fashioned, home-cooked meal."

"Isn't that great?" My father beamed.

The tow truck driver unchained his growling guard dog and patted her shiny black coat. "Come on, pup," he said. "Let's go home."

"Uh-huh," I mumbled, backing away from the "pup." "Great."

The tow truck driver's name was Ed. He lived with his wife, Myrna, on the outskirts of town in a small blue ranch-style house. It had shag carpeting and a stuffed antelope hanging over the dining room table. Myrna was a hugger, not to mention a cheek pincher. Sweetie Pie — the big black Doberman who spent the whole meal whimpering under the table, begging for scraps — turned out to be a real . . . sweetie pie. And I had to admit, the food was good.

Okay, not just good. Amazing. Fresh, juicy, roasted chicken. Real mashed potatoes loaded with butter and chives. Chunky, homemade applesauce, crunchy asparagus, brandied cranberries, and a loaf of soft, fluffy bread straight out of the oven. After a month and a half of greasy burgers, wilted salads, and stale burritos, it tasted like the best food I'd ever eaten.

After dinner, it was time for a tour of Ed and Myrna's basement, also known as the Roseland Showcase of Historical Barbed Wire and Geological Curiosities. That meant four walls lined with hundreds of strands of barbed wire — and ten tables covered with rocks.

"This type of wire was invented in 1897," Myrna said excitedly, pointing to a strand that looked exactly like every other strand of barbed wire I'd ever seen.

"Helvite rocks are very unusual in this region of New Mexico," Ed was saying on the other side of the room. He held up a brown rock the size of a baseball. "We found this one in a construction site about twenty miles outside of town."

Even Kirsten couldn't force herself to act interested. And Jake, of course, was up in the living room, listening to a baseball game. Dillie was in too good a mood to care what was happening, because we were due to visit Roswell the next day. Caleb and I just nodded along, pretending to listen.

But our parents weren't faking their oohs and ahs. I could tell by the way my parents trailed after Myrna like eager puppies, by the way Dillie's mother actually stopped talking for five seconds and listened to someone else's lecture, by the way the Schwebers . . . Well, Caleb's parents looked pretty much the same as they always did. They weren't very excitable.

"If they like this, just imagine what they'd think of Evelyn's collection!" Myrna told Ed.

"Who's Evelyn?" my father asked.

"Evelyn's our local historian, of sorts," Ed explained. "Our librarian, and archivist, and all-around collector. Rocks, bottles, old signs, restaurant menus, stories — you name it, Evelyn collects it."

"You folks want to know the *real* story of this

country out here, Evelyn's the first, last, and only lady you need to see," Myrna added. "She's the voice of Route 66."

Uh-oh. There was that word again. *Real.* I could almost see my parents' ears perking up.

"Would this Evelyn be willing to talk to us?" Dillie's mother asked eagerly.

"Can't imagine why not," Myrna said. "You could drive over tomorrow, if you can all fit into your two cars while Ed's fixing the third. She's about thirty miles down the road."

Dillie stiffened. "Mom —"

"That would be wonderful!" Dillie's mother said. "Thank you so much."

"Mom!" Dillie said again, louder. "We're supposed to go to Roswell tomorrow. Remember?"

"That's right," my father said. "I nearly forgot. No need for you all to be stuck here while our car gets fixed. You can ride over to Roswell and we'll meet you in a couple days in Santa Rosa."

"And miss the chance to meet the 'Voice of Route 66'?" Professor Kaplan's narrow eyebrows flew up her forehead. "Dillie, dear, I'm afraid we're just going to have to skip Roswell this time around."

"But can't we just go the next day?" Dillie asked.

"You know we're on a tight schedule," her mother said. "Now, let's just —"

"You *promised*!" Dillie shouted.

"Delia!" Professor Kaplan hissed, looking scandalized. "We're guests in this house. Behave yourself!"

Caleb's father cleared his throat. "Maybe we could pile the kids into our car, take them on their little side trip —"

"No." Dillie's mother shook her head. "Dillie's mature enough to understand that sometimes she needs to compromise. After all, whole world doesn't revolve around what she wants to do. Right, Dillie?"

Tears streamed down Dillie's face. But she nodded.

I couldn't stand it anymore. This was so unfair. After everything Dillie had done for me, there had to be *something* I could do for her.

"Why doesn't Kirsten drive us?" The words were out of my mouth before I'd even thought them through. Caleb and Dillie turned to gape at me. Professor Kaplan looked even more surprised.

"Kirsten?" she asked.

"I have my license," Kirsten said quickly. "And you *did* say I could get some driving practice on this trip." She locked eyes with me and smiled. "I can do it."

"I'm not sure we're comfortable sending you off to a strange town, with three kids to keep an eye on," Professor Novak said.

"We're not kids," I argued. "We'll totally behave. This is the *one thing* Dillie has cared about on this entire trip. She should get to go."

"I don't know." Professor Novak didn't sound convinced. "Kirsten, this would be a big responsibility."

"I can help," Jake said, appearing on the staircase. "Keep an eye on everyone, you know?"

My eyes couldn't bug out any wider. Caleb looked like he was about to fall over. Dillie had at least stopped crying.

Professor Kaplan sighed. "I wish I could say yes, I really do. But I just don't see how it will work. Even if we could all fit in one car and give you the other, you're not authorized to drive our rental car — and I'm sure Mr. Schweber doesn't want you driving his new SUV."

Mr. Schweber looked apologetic, but he didn't disagree.

Ed and Myrna exchanged a glance. "That's where I think we might be able to help you out,"

Ed said. He smiled at Dillie. "Trust me, little lady. I don't think you're going to be disappointed."

"It's, um . . . wow," Caleb said. His mouth opened again, but nothing came out.

I knew exactly how he felt. "Wow" pretty much said it all.

"It's perfect!" Dillie squealed. She threw her arms around Ed and Myrna. Then she grabbed her mother and squeezed tight. "Thank you, thank you, thank you!"

"Just make sure you stay out of trouble," Professor Kaplan said, disengaging herself.

"I have to drive *that*?" Kirsten mumbled under her breath.

"I have to *ride* in it?" Jake whispered.

"Isn't it perfect?" Dillie exclaimed.

"It's . . ." I glanced at Caleb, but his face was a total blank. "It's definitely the perfect vehicle for a trip to alien central," I said finally.

And that was one hundred percent the truth.

Ed's old car — "Just something I like to fix up on weekends" — wasn't a car at all. It was a van. Specifically, a snub-nosed Volkswagen bus. It was painted a faded grass green and slathered with pink and purple flowers and swirls. "Myrna painted it when we were kids," he explained. "Can't bear to paint over it."

"You can *never* paint over it," Dillie said in a hushed voice, running her fingers along one of the neon-purple blossoms. "It's a work of art."

Ed slapped a hand down on the hood. "You kids just take good care of her. Especially you, young lady," he told Kirsten.

"I'm an excellent driver," she said in her very best I'm-so-mature voice. "But . . . does it actually run?"

"You treat her well, she'll get you where you need to go," Ed said. "Just promise me one thing."

I realized he was talking to me, like I was the one in charge. I guess this *had* all been my idea. So I nodded. "Anything."

"If you meet any aliens up there in Roswell, you make sure to invite them back here for a nice, home-cooked dinner."

Chapter Nine

Location: Roswell, New Mexico
Population: 45,293
Miles Driven: 2,147
Days of Torment: 47

"This is it!" Dillie exclaimed as we rolled slowly through streets crowded with aliens. Or, at least, earthlings dressed up in really elaborate alien costumes. Tourists swarmed around us, most decked out in UFO shirts and tin foil hats, but some looking just like our parents: baggy PTA T-shirts, khaki shorts pulled up too high, fanny packs, and mom-hair.

"This is it." Kirsten carefully eased the van into a tight parallel parking space. "Out."

"It's amazing," Dillie breathed.

I looked out at the Star Tours visitor information stand, the Alien Invasion arcade, and Unidentified Frying Objects, a stir-fry joint. "It's something," I agreed.

"So?" Jake said. "Where are the UFOs?"

Dillie shot him a poisonous glare. He glared right back. I wondered if he was thinking about the Night of the Skunk. I had to slap a hand over my mouth to cover a wicked smile.

It turned out we'd picked the right day to come to Roswell. A banner hanging across the main street announced the 2ND ANNUAL OUT-OF-THIS-WORLD FESTIVAL. A band (Arnie and the Aliens) was playing in the town square, green antennae sprouting from their heads. Marathon runners with three eyes and four arms and *Star Wars* masks loped down the streets. And then there was the Alien Pet Parade. Dillie dragged us to the front of the crowd, gaping and cooing at the fluffy terrier with his fur dyed green, the turtle with his shell papered in aluminum foil, the ferret with googly eyes strapped to his torso, and the Chihuahua. (That one didn't need a costume; it looked like an alien all by itself.) Jake was still sulking, but he kept his mouth shut.

"Let's check out the laser show!" Dillie urged us, once the grand prize went to a poodle wearing orange goggles and purple antennae. (I'd been rooting for the Chihuahua.)

"Look at you, you're like a puppy," Kirsten said to her sister, laughing. "You might as well be running around with your tongue hanging out and your tail wagging."

Dillie blushed. "Don't you think it's cool?"

"*I* think it's cool," I assured her. Though mostly, I thought it was cool how excited she was. I'd never been that excited about anything. But you couldn't *make* yourself be like that. You were either like Dillie, the kind of person who saw the world in this totally weird, wonderful, unique way . . .

Or you weren't.

My whole life, I had spent so much time worrying that I might say or do something dumb, that people might figure out I was weird, that there was something different about me. It never occurred to me to worry that there *wasn't.*

"You guys go ahead to the laser show," I said, suddenly needing to be on my own. "I'm going to check out the town a little more."

"You sure?" Caleb asked. "Everything okay?"

I gave him a big smile. "Everything's awesome. I just don't feel like sitting. Too much car time, you know?"

"I don't know," Kirsten said nervously. "I promised your parents —"

"She'll be fine," Dillie said. I gave her a grateful smile.

"One hour, then meet back here," Kirsten told me. "*Don't* be late."

Once they were gone, I wandered through the crowds, feeling totally invisible. I started walking aimlessly, snapping a picture whenever I spotted a particularly good costume. After a few random turns, I found myself on a small, empty street, with only a single storefront: the Desert Sands Art Gallery.

The gallery was like something from a different planet. Outside, all I could see were aliens, and neon, and rhinestone-bedazzled ashtrays shaped like UFOs. But inside, it was SoHo and Paris and Rome all at once. People dressed all in black, talking in quiet voices about art and poetry and philosophy. Stark white walls, each featuring a single photograph.

I spun in place, trailing my eyes from one photo to the next. It was like the photographer had forced the desert itself down on the canvas. Somehow, the pictures were even more beautiful — more *real* — than the real thing. And that's when I finally got it, what it meant to be *real.* Why it mattered. It was all in the photos.

As opposed to the desert photos I'd taken. The best of them were cheesy and generic, like something you'd hang in a motel bathroom. The worst — the ones where I'd tried to be artsy, tipping the camera on a diagonal or turning on the night flash in stark daylight — looked like something you'd flush down a motel toilet. Then there were the goofy ones, destined for the *Journal of Torment*, but they didn't even count.

"You like?" a woman asked from behind me.

I turned around. She was probably about my mom's age, but if you didn't look closely, you'd figure she was a lot younger. Maybe it was the sleek black dress with a silver chain belt, and the dangly turquoise earrings that brushed her shoulders. Or maybe it was just the look on her face, like she was about to let you in on a secret joke.

"You look surprised," she said.

"I just didn't expect to find a place like this in . . . well, a place like this."

The woman sighed. "I get that a lot. Roswell may be about aliens and UFOs, but trust me, it isn't *all* we're about. So what do you think of the pictures?"

"I love them. Especially that one." I pointed to a black-and-white shot of a natural rock formation. It spurted out of the ground like a stone geyser. The dark shadow it cast on the bleached white sand looked like a hole through the center of the earth.

She smiled. "That's my favorite, too. Took me all day to get the light just right."

My eyes bugged out. "*You* took these?"

The woman nodded.

I swallowed the first question that popped into my head: *Why would someone like* you *bother talking to someone like* me*?*

"Are you a photographer?" she asked, after too many seconds had gone by without me saying anything.

"Me?" I shook my head.

"So what's that?" she asked, her eyes darting to the camera hanging around my neck.

"Oh, that? I mean, it's a camera. But it doesn't — I take pictures, but that doesn't make me. You know. A photographer."

"Actually, that's exactly what it does," she said.

"I just mean . . . I don't take pictures like *that*," I told her, sweeping my arms out to include the whole gallery.

She laughed. "I should hope not! That's the job of a photographer. To show people what the world looks like to you, and no one else."

"I guess I never thought about it that way," I admitted. "When I see stuff like this — the desert, or the mountains, or anything that's so amazing you have to get it on film, I try. But in the picture, it always just looks . . . small. Like anyone could have taken it. I want to take pictures that only *I* could take." I'd never really said it out loud before, never even thought it. But once the words were out, they felt true.

"Well, you're definitely thinking like an artist," the woman said. "That's the first step. The rest will come with time."

"Oh, I'm not an artist," I said quickly. "My friend Mina, *she's* the artist. I'm just . . ." I stopped.

I wanted to explain to her how it was, how Mina was the artsy one and Sam was the cool, stylish one, and I was — but that's where I ran out of steam. I didn't know what my thing was. According to Dillie and Caleb, I used to be the wild one, the fun one — but that was before. These days, I didn't *have* a thing. I was just there. And that's not something you want to admit to a stranger.

I shrugged. "I just like to take pictures," I said finally. "It's not art. It's only a way to remember things."

"There's nothing 'only' about that," the woman said. "Remembering, recording, retelling — it's how we understand the world. It's important."

"Well . . . maybe *your* pictures are important," I said. "But —"

"They're important to *me*," she said. "You want to be a photographer?" She held up a hand and shushed me before I could argue. "Take pictures that are important to *you*. Find a way to tell *your* story."

"I don't even know if I have a story," I admitted.

She grinned, and the I-have-a-secret look was back. "Everyone has a story. Some people just take a while to figure that out."

"You sure you have enough room?" I asked nervously as Kirsten backed the van up a few inches, careful not to hit the Buick bumper behind her. We were standing on the curb, waving her backward and forward, so she'd be sure not to knock into either of the cars pinning her in. I watched the narrow space between the cars and the van, trying to put it together in my head like a geometry problem. But every time, I kept coming around to the same solution — the van was trapped.

"I can do this," Kirsten insisted. She spun the wheel and inched forward again. "Just tell me before I go too far!"

"She can't do this," Dillie murmured. "She practically failed her driving test because of the parallel parking. There's no way."

"She *can*," I said firmly. After all the wheedling and whining we'd done to get permission for this trip, we were not admitting defeat.

"You got it!" Jake shouted, pumping a fist in the air as Kirsten slid the van out of the parking space.

She turned the wheel, starting a three-point turn on the dead-end street. "Now just let me turn this thing around and I'll —"

There was a long, guttural crunching noise. Then a popping and crackling sound like a giant bowl of Rice Krispies.

Kirsten was frozen at the wheel. "What . . . was . . . that?" she gasped.

Caleb and Jake darted behind the van to see what she had run over.

"It's not a person or anything," Jake reported.

"Not even a jackrabbit!" Caleb added. He

rejoined us on the curb. Kirsten climbed out of the van. She was a pale, sickly white color. "It was just some big cardboard boxes of stuff," Caleb explained.

"Stuff?" Kirsten repeated, her voice rising to supersonic range. "*Stuff?* What kind of *stuff*? And why was it in the *middle of the road*?"

Jake cleared his throat. "It wasn't exactly in the middle of the road," he pointed out. "It was actually, uh, on the sidewalk. You kind of . . . missed the road. Just a little."

Kirsten sank to the ground. She dropped her head between her knees. "Uhhh," she moaned. "Mom's going to *kill* me."

I patted her shoulder, feeling kind of awkward. "It'll be okay, Kirsten."

"Actually, Mom really will kill her," Dillie said.

"Dillie!" Caleb and I shouted together.

"I should have known this would happen," Kirsten said, tears beading at the corners of her eyes. "Of course something would go wrong. Everything always goes wrong!"

I'd never seen Kirsten like this. She was totally out of control. "It's not that bad," I tried.

"It's *worse*!" She shuddered. "My life is just one big disaster. First Thomas breaks up with me, then —"

"Thomas broke up with you?" Dillie asked, eyes wide. "When?"

Kirsten burst into tears. "Two weeks ago."

"Why didn't you tell me?" Dillie asked, sounding half offended and half worried.

It was like Kirsten hadn't even heard her. "He said we'd be together forever, and then —" She hiccuped, and wiped the edge of her shirt across her dripping nose. "And then I go away for two months and he basically forgets all about me. And now *this*!"

Jake was inspecting the bumper of the van. "There are no dents," he reported. "You can't even tell you hit anything."

"But the boxes . . ." Kirsten groaned.

"Maybe it was just trash," I said. "You know, recycling or something no one wanted —"

"My aliens!" The high-pitched shriek echoed up and down the street.

Uh-oh.

"Okay, maybe *someone* wanted them," I murmured. As an angry-looking woman came racing toward us, I hauled Kirsten off the ground. We were going to have to deal with this, one way or another.

"The aliens!" the woman screamed, kneeling by the smashed cardboard boxes. She ran her hands through her frizzy red hair, until it was nearly standing on end. "You killed them!"

The blood drained out of Kirsten's face. "I . . . killed . . . ?"

"Aliens?" Dillie mouthed, just as pale as her sister.

The woman stood up, smoothing down her flowing flowered skirt. Her hair, on the other hand, stayed just as wild and alarmed as she was. "It's ruined," she murmured, fists clenched. "All ruined."

"I'm so sorry," Kirsten said quickly. She wiped away a tear. "I don't know what was in those boxes, but —"

"I told you, those are our aliens," the woman said. "Or at least they *were* our aliens." She sighed. "I knew I shouldn't have left them alone on the sidewalk. But it was just for a few minutes, and . . ."

Caleb cleared his throat. "Um, excuse me, but are you saying there were, uh, real, live aliens in those boxes?"

The woman looked at Caleb like he was insane. "Of course not." She rolled her eyes at us, as if to say, *Who is this lunatic?* "They were props for tonight's show. We're performing at the festival, or at least we were —"

"You're Luna Moonbeam!" Dillie exclaimed. "I *love* your music." She started fumbling in her pockets, pulling out a crumpled receipt and a stub of pencil. She shoved them at the woman. "Can I have your autograph?"

"Um, Dillie," I whispered, "we've kind of got bigger issues right now."

"But this is Luna Moonbeam, as in Luna and the Light Brigade!" Dillie said eagerly. "Their live bootleg recording from the Are You Out There? Convention is legendary. They're famous for these mechanical alien props they have that actually dance and —" She broke off, staring sadly at the pile of smashed boxes. "Oh."

"I'm so, so sorry. I really am," Kirsten said, sounding like she was trying not to cry. "Please don't call my parents. They'll kill me. I'll do anything I can to fix this. Anything."

"We *have* to fix this," Dillie agreed. "The Out-of-This-World Fest can't go on without Luna and the Light Brigade."

Luna sighed. "You're right. But Luna and the Light Brigade can't go on without our aliens. They're our trademark."

"Can't you fix them?" Caleb asked.

"I certainly hope so," Luna said. "But not in time for the concert."

Kirsten plunged her head into her hands. "I'm going to be grounded for *life.*"

"Snap out of it, Kirsten!" I whispered. "There's got to be something we can do," I told Luna. "What if we figured out a way to help you put on your show?"

"Well, I don't see how you can do that," Luna said, "unless you can find me a ship full of aliens by five P.M."

Dillie's eyes lit up. I wondered if she was thinking the same thing I was.

"This is *Roswell,*" I reminded Luna, as a crazy idea bubbled into my brain. "You want aliens? We'll get you aliens."

* * *

Location: Center stage

Population: 5 band members, 5 "aliens"

Miles Driven: 2,147

Days of Torment: 47, plus one very, very long hour under the spotlight

I cannot believe I'm doing this, I thought. *I cannot believe I'm doing this and not* hating *it.*

We'd found Luna and the Light Brigade some aliens. Five of them. True, we couldn't replace the elaborate mechanical models that had taken months to create. But we'd offered them a different kind of alien, lifelike and life-size. The Light Brigaders had accepted gratefully.

(Jake had accepted the proposal slightly *less* gratefully. "You're doing it," I'd said. He shook his head. "Yes," I'd said. "No." That's when Caleb stepped up. "You do this, and tomorrow I'll convince my parents that you're sick enough you have to stay in the motel all week and watch baseball games." And just like that, Jake was in.)

It only took half an hour to beg and borrow some haphazard costumes off the tourists and gift shop managers clogging the streets. Soon we had more antennae, fake arms, bug eyes, blue wigs, and neon tutus than anyone could ever want. We spent another forty-five minutes rehearsing our parts.

And then it was showtime. There we were, under the spotlight. Wearing silver body paint and sparkly, wiggling antennae. Staring out at an audience of three hundred alien-worshippers.

On the plus side, we didn't have to play any serious instruments. This was lucky, since none of us had any musical talent whatsoever. (Except Kirsten, who played the pipe organ for some reason, and Jake, who claimed to play Expert level on Guitar Hero.) Dillie and Caleb were given tambourines, Kirsten snapped a pair of castanets, Jake got two plastic maracas — and I was stuck with a triangle. "Just strike it whenever you want," Luna had urged me. "We're flexible."

The band was less flexible about the dance we were supposed to do, imitating their famous alien machines. We had to wave our arms up and down and kick our feet out, Rockette style — but do it all as mechanically as possible, like some kind of robots from outer space.

I thought it would be terrifying to stand up onstage in front of hundreds of fans, wearing my antennae, banging on my triangle, swinging my hips back and forth in an alien hula dance.

And it was terrifying — for the first few seconds.

But then the spotlights blinded me to the crowd, and Luna's guitar chords blasted through the speakers. Somehow, I forgot to be terrified or humiliated. I forgot to do anything but dance. I had to admit, the band was better than I'd expected. Soon the whole crowd was singing along — and I couldn't help it. I joined in.

I'm an alien from outer space,
Spying on the human race!
Swooping down from up above,
Found your Earth and fell in love!

Okay, so it was even cheesier than the time my Hebrew school class put on a Hanukkah musical starring the the Amazing Dreidel and his sidekick, the Incredible Singing Potato Latke. But when the audience burst into applause, it felt pretty good.

Caleb and Dillie were asleep in the back of the van. Jake was listening to a baseball game and glaring at the back of my head. He'd been giving us the silent treatment all afternoon, still mad that we'd made him wear the orange tutu.

Not that I was paying attention to Jake. I was not. And would not. Ever again.

I was sitting in the front seat next to Kirsten, pretending to navigate. But we were driving through empty miles of desert wilderness; there wasn't much need for maps. This road was basically our only option. Kirsten was still a little shaky after the parallel-parking alien massacre. I think she just wanted someone else telling her what to do, for once.

"Fnk oo," she mumbled, keeping her eyes pinned on the road.

"What?"

She made a sucking-on-a-lemon face. "Thank you."

"Oh." After the performance, Kirsten had immediately gone back into I'm-better-than-you mode. Saying thank-you wasn't really her style. "You're welcome?"

"No, really," she said. "You saved me."

"It was all of us," I pointed out.

"It was *you*," Kirsten argued. "*You* came up with the idea, and *you* talked that Luna woman into going along with it." She shook her head. "You were, like, some kind of evil genius. Only not actually evil."

I grinned. "Never doubt the Lizard Queen," I murmured.

"What?"

"Nothing." But it wasn't nothing.

"I really owe you one," Kirsten said.

I suspected that Dillie would be able to come up with the perfect way for Kirsten to pay us back. Or maybe I would come up with it myself. Apparently, that was the kind of thing I did now.

"Hey, Kirsten, I'm really sorry about Thomas," I said. In all the chaos, I'd almost forgotten the news about her big secret breakup.

"Who?"

"Uh, Thomas? Your boyfriend? I mean ex — I mean. You know. *Thomas*."

"Oh." Kirsten's fingers tightened around the wheel. "Whatever. He was totally immature, anyway. You know?" She laughed, though it sounded kind of fake. "I guess you don't know. You're just a kid, after all."

Same old Kirsten. Even after breaking up with her boyfriend, crashing the van, having a nervous breakdown, and turning into an alien, she hadn't changed at all.

But maybe I had.

Chapter Ten

Location: Grand Canyon, Arizona
Population: 5 million tourists per year
Miles Driven: 2,310
Days of Torment: 51

The next few days passed in a blur of national parks, Technicolored diners, and miles and miles of cactus-studded desert. (And because it kept getting hotter and hotter, a blur of motel pools — some that we even had official permission to use.) In between all the tourist spots were miles and miles of empty desert and a scattering of very, very empty towns. Ramshackle gas stations with 1950s-style pumps. Fading Route 66 museums with crumbling plaster dinosaurs and broken neon signs. Abandoned town squares with cacti growing in the middle of the street.

I'd never seen so much dusty brown emptiness.

But then we hit Arizona's Painted Desert, which was lit up in a rainbow of colors, rocks striped with reds and purples and oranges. I took a bunch of pictures, knowing I was never going to be able to capture the real thing. But I had to try. It glowed in the afternoon sun, as we all just stared down at it, totally silent. There are some things you don't talk about, because they're too big — and when you try to put them into words, they just get small.

The Grand Canyon was like that, too. At first, it was kind of disappointing. I'd always figured the Grand Canyon would be, you know — a *canyon*. But it turned out the Grand Canyon was so grand that from one side of it, you couldn't see the other. So it looked more like an incredibly steep cliff, sloping down and out into a vast, reddish orange nothingness.

It was still beautiful.

We watched the sun set, dipping down into the canyon and lighting the sky on fire before it disappeared.

We probably shouldn't have sat there for *quite* so long watching the sky fade to black, while all the other tourists drifted away. Because when we finally stood up, it was pitch-dark — and we'd missed the last shuttle ride back to the campground.

"I told you to keep an eye on your watch!" Professor Kaplan admonished her husband.

He sighed wearily. And then, for the first time, he talked back. "You also told me to keep an eye on the children and keep an eye on the edge and keep an eye on the woman from Idaho you thought might be trying to steal your backpack. I only have so many eyes, dear."

It was too dark to see Professor Kaplan's expression, but I could imagine it. And from the sound of Dillie's muffled giggling, so could she.

We inched single file along the trail that wound along the canyon rim, with Professor Kaplan leading the way and Jake bringing up the rear as usual. Cell phones lit our way . . . barely. Ten minutes into our tortoise-paced hike, Jake screamed. And when we turned around, he was gone.

We panicked.

Everyone turned toward the edge, peering over, the same horrified question slashing through our minds. Was it possible that he . . . ?

"Ugh!" Kirsten exclaimed, aiming her dimly lit cell phone screen at a large boulder. Jake perched behind it, smirking. Kirsten snorted in disgust. "You are *so* immature."

The adults started yelling a lot of *You scared us half to death!* and *What were you thinking?* and *Never do that again!* while Dillie, Caleb, and I tried to stay out of the way.

"What a jerk," Dillie murmured.

"Tell me about it," Caleb agreed.

"We really should have thought of that ourselves," Dillie added enviously.

I grinned. "Tell me about it."

Before the yelling went too far, a ranger truck pulled up alongside us. We all piled in and got a bumpy ride back to our campsite, where Jake's punishment was having to cook us all hot dogs and grilled cheese. It might have been the best-tasting meal of the trip.

The campground didn't have a view of the canyon, or the desert, or anything but a bunch of trailers and the donkey corral. "People ride those down to the bottom of the canyon," Caleb explained. "Maybe tomorrow we can —"

"No," my mother said quickly. *"No donkeys."*

It turned out my mom had tried to do that once, when she was a younger. But when she'd tried to climb onto the donkey, it had tipped and fallen on top of her. "Never again," she vowed. On the one hand, this was too bad, because a donkey trail ride sounded kind of fun.

On the other hand, the donkeys smelled like fertilizer.

* * *

Location: Chupacabra, Arizona
Population: 224
Miles Driven: 2,366
Days of Torment: 52

We were about twenty miles from the California border when I decided it was time to finish the *Journal of Torment* and send it on its way. I'd been holding on to it so that I could fit in as much of the trip as possible — but if I didn't send each copy soon, I'd make it back to the East Coast before either copy did. Fortunately, Dillie and Kirsten were out having a special Kaplan-Novak family night with their parents, leaving me all alone in the motel room.

I lay down on the saggy mattress, soaking in the quiet. No parents, no Dillie and Caleb, no bossy sisters or annoyingly cute cousins, no Family Entertainment Hour. And for a moment, it was blissful.

Then it was just boring.

So I started flipping through my latest stack of photos. I'd developed them at a twenty-four-hour place in Sedona. Many of them — too many — were just lame shots of the desert. They were pictures anyone could have taken.

But then there were the other pictures:

- Dillie and Caleb in the Texas ghost town, dressed as a sheriff and her prisoner.
- Caleb in alien antennae, the sun glinting off his silver face-paint.
- Jake, his back to the camera, his earbuds in his ears, slouched against a dying tree.
- Kirsten doing a lipstick pout in front of the mirror, her eyes twinkling in the reflection.
- A close-up of Dillie's flaring nostrils, as she stuck her tongue out at the camera.

I laughed as I got to one of the more recent ones, a shot of Dillie and Caleb crawling into the hollow of a large rock. I'd bet them a milk shake that they couldn't both fit inside. Sam and Mina were never going to believe all the stuff I did this summer. And they were *never* going to believe that some of it was even my idea. I looked at the picture of myself in full-on Elvis gear and smiled.

After all, Liza Gold didn't do that kind of thing. Liza Gold was afraid of embarrassment and humiliation and anything that might make anyone stare at her, eyes bugged out, thinking, *That girl is* so *uncool.*

Lizard, on the other hand, was fearless.

Suddenly, I slapped the notebook shut. The elaborately drawn letters on the cover spelled out *Journal of Torment*, in bright purple and green. But that wasn't right. Or maybe it was, I thought, remembering Family Entertainment Hour. Torment was definitely part of this summer's story. It just wasn't the whole story. It wasn't the right one. Just like these weren't the right souvenirs.

Not for Sam and Mina, at least.

I'd already decided I would get them something else when we reached California, maybe some cool sunglasses or one of those bead necklaces that surfers were always wearing in the movies. Something pretty I could give them in person when we were all home again. But for the official souvenir, I needed something special — a way to stuff my entire summer into an envelope, so they could understand.

I dug up the two padded envelopes I'd bought, each large enough to contain one handmade *Journal of Torment.* Then I found the two lizard cowboys Caleb had given me, and wrapped each of them in several layers of tissues. I was pretty sure he wouldn't mind me passing the lizards on to my two best friends. It was for a good cause. I was introducing them to the new-and-improved Liza. Liza the fearless, Liza the weird . . . Liza the Lizard Queen.

I slipped one of the lizards into each envelope. Then I paged through my photos again, looking for the perfect shots. For Sam, the picture from the Hound Dog Hotel — I was waving at the camera, my fluffed-up pompadour poufing over Dillie's oversize sunglasses. For Mina, a picture from one of our pool trespassing trips. I was balancing at the very top of a fence, one flip-flop wedged into each side of the chain link, my hair soaking wet, my arms raised in triumph. I flipped the photos over and wrote the same thing on the back of each. *Wish you were here! Love, Lizard.*

I slipped the pictures into the envelopes and sealed them up. Then I started to laugh, picturing Sam's and Mina's faces when they unwrapped their souvenirs. They wouldn't get it — not until we were all back home and I could tell them about Dillie and Caleb, and about Jake, and about lizards, and about everything. Then they would get that things were different now, that *I* was different. And that at the same time, I was exactly the same. I was pretty sure they would get it all, because no matter who I was or how many weird costumes I wore, they were my best friends.

Getting it was just the kind of thing that best friends did.

* * *

Location: The desert
Population: 14 jackrabbits, 2 coyotes, 1 tortoise
Miles Driven: A lot more
Days of Torment: A lot . . . *less*?

Arizona was a lot of desert, but not *all* desert. There was also the Wigwam Motel, where we slept in giant concrete tepees and listened to a radio station that broadcast baseball games in Navajo. There was Meteor Crater, a 570-foot-deep hole in the ground that was about a mile wide and 50,000 years old. There was the Rattlesnake Zone, with one of the world's biggest collections of live rattlesnakes. "Why would anyone want the world's biggest collection of live rattlesnakes?" I asked. "Isn't *one* rattlesnake still too big a collection?" But when Dillie, Caleb, and I dared one another to hold one of the defanged rattlers, I was the only one with enough nerve to do it.

There were plenty of weird museums for our parents to enjoy — the toy soldier museum, the old teapot museum, the license plate museum, the museum that was just a bunch of dusty mannequins dressed up as famous people. There was yet another Mom's Café (the fifteenth one that we'd eaten at since starting out), but this one definitely had the best chicken pot pie west of the Mississippi.

And there were Dillie and Caleb, by my side. It was starting to feel like they always would be. But eventually we crossed the border into California, and after miles and miles of more desert, civilization returned. First it was just a few houses. Then a factory, and a bunch of outlet stores. Then, without warning, Los Angeles. It took us several smog-filled hours to battle our way through the traffic into the city itself, but then there we were. The Pacific Ocean. The end of the road.

Literally.

* * *

Location: Santa Monica, California
Population: 84,084
Miles Driven: 3,130
Days of (Not *Quite*) Torment: 55

Hot.

That was all I could think; *hot* was filling up my brain. But not the bad kind of hot. Not hot like sweaty T-shirts and burning metal doors and sticky skin peeling off vinyl car seats. Not hot like shimmering waves rising from concrete, like scratchy throats and a single bottle of puke-warm water cooked by the sun.

It was hot sand between bare toes. Hot towels laid out on a gently sloping beach. Hot sunlight bouncing off arms and legs slathered in super-SPF sunscreen. Hot that made ice cream melt down the cone before you could get it in your mouth. It was the kind of hot that made you desperate to run headlong into the surf, plunge into the frigid Pacific, then burst out again, dripping and shivering under the bright sun. It was the kind of hot that made you tired, even though all you'd done all day was lie down.

"We should find some shade," I said, squinting up at the cloudless sky.

"Uh-huh," Caleb said, stretched out on his towel.

Dillie just sighed and turned over. She'd been flipping through some trashy celebrity magazine, but now it lay beside her on the sand.

"We really should," I said, too lazy to move.

"Uh-huh," Caleb said again.

I closed my eyes, enjoying the feel of the sun on my face. "This is the best day ever."

"Better than the Jesse James Wax Museum?" Caleb joked.

"Better."

"Not better than the Tee Pee Trading Post?" Dillie said.

"*Twice* as better."

"That doesn't even make sense," Caleb said.

"It's not grammatical," I argued. "But it still makes sense."

Dillie fumbled for the cooler and pulled out a soda, without opening her eyes. She popped it open, sighing along with the cool hiss of carbonation. "*Maybe* the best day ever." She propped herself up on her elbow, just high enough to gulp down the cool drink. "Okay, definitely."

My parents had delivered on their promise. At the end of the road, we had three days of ultra-*normal* vacation. Three days of sun and fun at the Oceancrest Resort in Santa Monica, California. No sights to see, no regional food to sample, no people to meet. Nothing to do but lie in the sand and listen to the sound of the ocean lapping at the shore.

There was just one problem: My family was the

only one staying. The beach vacation was a special Gold Family favor to me, not part of the official group trip. In a few hours, Caleb's and Dillie's families were heading to the airport — which meant this was the end. I wasn't sorry to say good-bye to gasoline fumes and car sickness and meat loaf. But I couldn't imagine saying good-bye to Caleb and Dillie.

Not that I wasn't excited to get home and see my friends. When we got to the hotel in Santa Monica, my souvenirs from Sam and Mina were waiting at the front desk. Mina's package was tiny, and wrapped in this cool, vintage paper. Even the envelope looked artsy, covered in all her little drawings. Just seeing her handwriting made me remember how much I missed her. And I missed her even more when I opened up the package to discover a funky bracelet that would go perfectly with my favorite tank top. It was the kind of thing I would have seen someone else wearing (someone like Mina) and wished I could have — but would never have picked out for myself.

The box from Sam was a lot bigger, with strips of tape slapped over all the edges to make sure it didn't bust open on the way. I tore it open and squealed in excitement. (Everyone in the hotel lobby turned to gape at me, but I didn't care. Once you've dressed up like an alien in front of several hundred gawking tourists, a few lobby gapers don't seem like such a big deal.) It was a beach care package: a shell necklace, a pair of mismatched flip-flops, and a green T-shirt that read I'D RATHER BE SURFING IN SALT ISLE. For a second, I was jealous, imagining Sam spending the summer surfing the waves and lounging on the beach. No highway food for her, no boring museums or skeezy motels.

But then I remembered all the other things my summer had been about, and I wasn't jealous at all. A few days at the beach would be great — especially now that I had my new flip-flops — but I wouldn't have wanted to switch places with Sam or Mina. My summer turned out to be perfect, just the way it was. The only unperfect thing about it was that it had to end.

Soon.

I forced myself to sit up. We were running out of daylight hours, and by the time the sun hit the water, Caleb and Dillie would be gone. Besides, I wanted to do this now, while we were on our own. Our parents were sitting under oversize umbrellas down the beach, the way parents do. Kirsten was there, too. After our trip to Roswell she'd spent a day or two hanging out with us, but pretty soon it was back to the grown-up table. Since she'd started bossing us around again, none of us were that sad to see her go. Jake, on the other hand, was . . . Well, I wasn't sure where Jake was. Last I saw him, he'd been hanging around some group of pretty blond girls, pretending to care about their dog. For all I knew, they'd kidnapped him and turned him into their full-time pet groomer. Or maybe they'd gotten so sick of his constant baseball chatter that they'd buried him in the sand.

I don't know and I don't care, I reminded myself. Jake was old news.

"I got something for you guys," I said to Dillie and Caleb, pulling their going-away gifts out of my backpack.

Caleb sat up, surprised. "You shouldn't have."

"Well, technically I guess I didn't," I said. "I *made* them for you."

Dillie clapped. "An arts and crafts project? A Lizzie Lizard original? Hand it over."

I gave one to each of them, a little nervous about what they would think.

"On three?" Dillie suggested to Caleb.

He nodded. "One . . . two . . ."

Dillie ripped open the wrapping paper long before Caleb got to three.

"Hey!" Caleb protested. But he was already tearing his own present out of the paper.

When the wrapping paper was balled up in the sand, they both gaped at me.

"Wow," Dillie breathed. She ran a hand lightly over the cover of the notebook, like she was making sure it was real.

Caleb flipped through the pages, his eyes getting wider and wider. "Liza, it's . . . it's . . ."

"You like it?" I said hopefully. I'd pasted new covers onto the notebooks. No more *Journal of Torment.* Now the cover of each read *Cross-Country with Dillie, Caleb, and the Lizard Queen.* Each page was filled with photographs of the three of us, running wild across the country.

"It's perfect," Dillie said. "More than perfect."

"There's no such thing as more than perfect," Caleb said. "That's just what it is. Perfect."

"Super-perfect!" Dillie tried, ignoring him. "Perfect plus!"

"I don't have anything for you," Caleb said sadly, turning back to me.

"*I* give you the gift of my presence," Dillie said. "Well, for at least" — she checked her watch — "forty-eight more minutes."

* * *

Forty-eight minutes had never passed so quickly. But there we were, standing outside the hotel lobby. Saying good-bye.

"I'll miss you," I said.

Dillie snorted. "Like you missed us last time? By forgetting everything we ever did together?"

"Not *exactly* like that," I promised. "Not this time."

"Don't look so glum, Lizard." Dillie slung an arm around my shoulder and another around Caleb's. "We'll see each other soon enough. Maybe next summer. After all, Kirsten's got her license, remember. Maybe we should do Route 66, the sequel!"

We all glanced over at Kirsten, who was primly shaking hands with all the grown-ups. She caught us watching and — so fast that none of the parents noticed — stuck out her tongue.

The three of us burst into laughter. "Maybe not," we agreed.

"Do you . . ." Caleb hesitated. His cheeks flushed pink and his eyes darted from one side to the other. "You want me to go find Jake so you can say good-bye to him, too?"

I knew exactly where Jake was. My Jake radar still pinged whenever he came near. I'd tried to shut it off, but there was nothing I could do.

Ping, ping, ping.

He was leaning against the hotel wall, trying to chat up a couple of pretty girls headed for the beach. If I were still speaking to him, I would point out that they were at least three years older than him. As far as they were concerned, he was probably just *some little kid.*

I decided to let him figure it out for himself.

"You're not going anywhere," I told Caleb. "Who knows when we'll see each other again? We might as well make this last thirty seconds count."

Dillie threw her arms around me and squeezed tight. "Thanks for an awesome summer, Lizard," she whispered. "Don't forget this."

"Never," I promised, hugging her back.

"Delia!" Professor Kaplan shouted, waving her toward the car. "No more dawdling, we're going to be late for the airport!"

Dillie sighed. "She means we're only going to be *three* hours early instead of *four* hours early. But when Professor Kaplan calls . . ." She put on a sparkling fake smile. "Coming, Mother dearest!" she yelled back, giving me another quick hug. And then she was gone.

Caleb was next. His cheeks flushed even

brighter. "So, um, my parents are talking about visiting some relatives in New Jersey this winter," he stammered. "I might see you kind of soon."

I was surprised by how excited I was at the thought.

Well, he wasn't . . . *un*-cute. He had pretty good hair, especially when it was all mussed and sticking up on his head. And the green of his eyes was freakishly bright behind the glasses. *Freakish* in a good way, I mean. He wasn't just some random boy who could be shoved into a category: cute, not-cute, sort-of-maybe-if-you-squint cute. He was Caleb. Just Caleb. Neat-freak, spacey, picky, persnickety, loyal, dependable, always-knew-the-right-thing-to-say-even-if-he-didn't-always-know-how-to-say-it *Caleb.*

Without warning, *Just Caleb* gave me a lightning-quick kiss on the cheek. Then, face bright red, head down, he ran away to join his parents.

After two months, I was finally alone. (Unless you counted my parents. I didn't.)

Did Caleb Schweber really just give me my first kiss?

Okay, not *kiss*-kiss. But . . .

I decided not to think about it. Not yet, at least. I would have plenty of time to figure things out.

(And tell Sam and Mina about it. And overanalyze. And obsess over every single, tiny, potentially crucial detail.)

But not now. Instead, I grabbed my camera from my bag and started snapping pictures. Of the Kaplan-Novaks' and the Schwebers' cars pulling out of the lot, with Caleb's and Dillie's faces pressed to the glass. Of my parents, huddling over a California guidebook, trying to find some kind of wacky and *real* tourist attraction to distract them from the beach. Of the road that stretched away from the hotel, winding toward the desert.

Find a way to tell your *story*, that photographer in Roswell had told me. And suddenly I didn't feel quite so alone. Maybe the summer was over; maybe Dillie and Caleb were gone. But my story — *Lizard's* story — was just getting started.

CHECK OUT THE OTHER BOOKS IN THE CANDY APPLE SUMMER TRILOGY!

Enjoy this special sneak peek at

by Lara Bergen

My mom rolled down the windows, and that unmistakable beachy smell filled the car: salt, sand, and even a little coconut oil mixed in. I took a deep breath. This beach road was a lot different than the ones in New Jersey that I was used to. Where were all the T-shirt shops and ice-cream stands? The amusement park? The arcade? All this place had were beach houses, as far as I could see.

"So, uh, where's the boardwalk?" I finally asked my mother.

"Oh, I don't think there is one, honey," she said.

"No boardwalk? So what do kids *do* here?" I asked her.

"Well . . ." She shrugged. "I guess they go to the beach."

Every day? For eight weeks?

Finally, we turned off the main road. Before I knew it, we were driving toward a big house with a sign on the front that said ISLE BE BACK.

"Is that it?" I asked my mother. "Wow, it's pretty cool! I mean, it doesn't look quite as huge as you described it, but that roof deck looks like fun. And it has a pool! And a tennis court, too?" I almost hated to admit it, but this place was going to be awesome!

"Huh?" my mom said absentmindedly. "Tennis court? Oh no, hon. That's not it." She laughed. Then she drove right by the house and pointed to another one behind it. "There you go. The Drift Inn. That's us."

I'd seen some big houses — Olivia Miner's came to mind — but this thing was out of control. Way bigger than the other house I'd been looking at. So big that there wasn't even *room* for a tennis court or pool around it. I'd assumed it was some kind of old hotel or school or something.

And by "old," I mean . . . a *total* mess.

Enjoy this special sneak peek at

by Denene Millner

There weren't any seats on the train, and because my hands were full with my art supplies and I wasn't used to riding a subway, I forgot to brace myself for takeoff. As soon as the train pulled out of the station, I went flying into a nearby girl wearing a hot-pink watch.

"Omigod, I'm so sorry," I told her, trying to catch my footing.

"Um, the poles are a perfect way to keep that from happening," the girl said. She giggled, so I guessed she hadn't meant to be mean. I still cringed.

"Nice art box," she added. "You an artist?"

I hesitated. I didn't really know what to say back, but I settled on a weak "Kinda."

"Actually, my niece is quite talented," Auntie Jill chimed in. I fought back a groan. "I see you have an art box, too — are you an artist?" she asked the girl.

"I want to be." The girl smiled warmly. "I'm actually on my way to the SoHo Children's Art Program. Today's my first day."

"Really? I'm an instructor there, and Mina is going to be in the camp, too," Auntie Jill said excitedly. "What's your name?"

"Gabriella," she said, rolling the "r" in her name and giving a little wave.

"See, Mina?" Auntie Jill said, turning toward me. "You've already made a new friend."

I tossed a halfhearted grin in the girl's direction, then focused my attention on my purple Converses. My best friends Sam and Liza had signed their names on the sides with special sparkly white marker, reminding me not to forget them while I was at my "fancy art camp."

But as for Gabriella? I wasn't sure if she'd be real friend material. Suddenly, I missed Liza and Sam more than ever.